I0744980

Black Shuck Books
www.blackshuckbooks.co.uk

First published in Great Britain in 2020 by
Black Shuck Books
Kent, UK

978-1-913038-58-8

Aurora

The social platform that shines
a light for everyone

by Jo M Thomas

BLACK
SHUCK
BOOKS

Download of Activity

Times adjusted to BST
Times rounded to nearest minute

Indirect interaction recorded No
Advertising removed Yes
Interaction blocks unbroken by page breaks Yes

Site Sign-up: 10:13
    Forename(s):   Siward
    Surname: Walls
    Age: <blank>
    Gender: Male
    Location: UK

    Harvested data – Recorded as "Configuration 0"
    Platform: Desktop / laptop
    Browser: Onion
    OS: Great Awk, GUI enabled
    Resolution: 1920 x 1080
    IP: <Hidden>
Suggested filters
    Location: UK (0)
    IT: Open Source (0)
                            Privacy (0)
                            Security (0)
                            Woggins (0)
    Narrative: Lone Hero (0)
                            Knowledge Wins (0)
                            Resourcefulness (0)
Flag:
    Timing: Typical core working hours = Mon-Fri, 09:00-
                            16:00 suggests "Unemployed", "Self-Employed",
                            "Shift Work", "Unconcerned Employee" or
                            "Relaxed Employer"

Prompt: Auto generated 10:14
Sign-up Welcome
    Hello Siward, and welcome to Aurora, the social platform that
    shines a light for everyone! We hope that you enjoy our
    community. Don't forget to fill in your profile with a little more
    detail to help people you may know identify you. Why don't you
    tell us what you're up to right now for your first post?

continues…

Daily Fortune Cookie
Filters applied:
Narrative: Lone Hero
                    Knowledge Wins
Suggests: Using Aurora

Nothing in life is to be feared, only to be understood.

INTERACTION — *LIKE*
Daily Fortune Cookie

Improving filters
Narrative: Lone Hero +1 (1)
                    Knowledge Wins +1 (1)

INTERACTION — *NAVIGATION MENU*
News > Top Ten Stories – Suggested for You
Filters Applied: General popularity
                          UK
                          IT

1. Queen's Speech clears Commons
2. NotBramble attacks about data not money
3. NI women to get free abortions on English NHS
4. The new laws of robotics?
5. Government data site user details leaked
6. BBC Radio 1 struggling to find talent
7. Hillsborough family disappointed
8. Best and worst shopping districts ranked
9. Free drugs for chronically ill?
10. Trump mocks TV host's facelift

INTERACTION — *CLICK-THROUGH*
NotBramble attacks about data not money

Improving filters
IT: Security +1 (1)

continues…

INTERACTION — *CLICK-THROUGH*
The new laws of robotics?

Suggested filters
    Technology: New & Developing (0)
    Genre: Science Fiction (0)

INTERACTION — *CLICK-THROUGH*
Government data site user details leaked

Improving filters
    IT: Privacy +1 (1)
    Security +1 (2)

Post: **10:16**
    NotBramble attacks about data not money
    Some useful detail here.

Improving filters
    IT: Security +1 (3)

INTERACTION — *NAVIGATION MENU*
Games > Top Five Games – Suggested for You
    Filters Applied: General popularity
    UK
    Narrative: Lone Hero

1. *Bubble Blast (Match 3, Casual)*
2. *Dragon's Nest (Simulation, Casual)*
3. *Texas Hold'em (Table, Casino)*
4. *Call of the Valkyrie (Role-playing, Action)*
5. *Monsters at Dawn (Action, Battle)*

INTERACTION — *CLICK-THROUGH*
Dragon's Nest | Info

Suggested filters
    Genre: Fantasy (0)

continues…

INTERACTION — *CLICK-THROUGH*
Call of the Valkyrie | Info

> *Improving filters*
> *Genre:*   *Fantasy +1 (1)*

INTERACTION — *CLICK-THROUGH*
Monsters at Dawn | Info

> *Improving filters*
> *Genre:*   *Fantasy +1 (2)*

Timeout: 11:07
No interaction for 30 minutes

Reply: **David Myttel 20:51**
NotBramble attacks about data not money
Poor technical understanding. This link is far more literate.

NotBramble targets specific files

Suggested connection: David Myttel (0)

Sign-in: **10:14**
Harvested data – Using Configuration 0
Flag:
> *Timing:*   *Typical core working hours = Mon-Fri, 09:00-16:00, suggests "Unemployed", "Self-Employed", "Shift Work", "Unconcerned Employee" or "Relaxed Employer"*

Prompt: **Auto generated 10:14**
Daily Sign-in Welcome
Hello Siward, and welcome back to Aurora, the social platform that shines a light for everyone! Don't forget to fill in your profile with a little more detail to help people you may know identify you. Why don't you tell us what you're up to right now for your first post of the day?

Post: **Auto generated 10:14**
Daily Fortune Cookie
Filters applied:
> *Narrative:*   *Resourcefulness*
> *Suggests:*   *Using Aurora*

New and rewarding opportunities are developing for you.

INTERACTION — *LIKE*
Daily Fortune Cookie

Improving filters
> *Narrative:*   *Resourcefulness +1 (2)*

INTERACTION — *CLICK-THROUGH*
<u>NotBramble targets specific files</u>

Improving filters
> *IT:*   *Security +1 (4)*

INTERACTION — *LIKE*
Reply to **<u>NotBramble attacks about data not money</u>**

---

continues…

NotBramble attacks about data not money
Poor technical understanding. This link is far more literate.

Thank you for the link. As you say, it's much more technical but I think they're ignoring the geopolitical aspects that the first link covers.

Suggested filters
    Interests: *Global Politics (0)*

Prompt: **Auto generated 10:42**
Help with Connections
Building Connections: David Myttel (0)

Do you know David? Or would you like to converse with him more often?

INTERACTION — *NAVIGATION MENU*

News > Top Ten Stories – Suggested for You
    Filters Applied: *General popularity*
                        UK
                        IT

1. *Council leader quits over tower block fire response*
2. *Security services call NotBramble cyberterrorism*
3. *Therapy in prison for sex offenders is failing*
4. *NHS to start over with a Woggin?*
5. *Big companies increasing security bug bounties*
6. *Funeral for inspirational arena victim*
7. *A Bramble by any other name?*
8. *Creator of Bramble offers to fight NotBramble*
9. *German MPs approve same sex marriage*
10. *Trump travel ban comes into effect*

INTERACTION — *CLICK-THROUGH*

Security services call NotBramble cyberterrorism

Improving filters
    IT: *Security +1 (5)*

---

continues…

INTERACTION — *CLICK-THROUGH*
  NHS to start over with a Woggin?

    Improving filters
      IT: *Open Source +1 (1)*
                              Woggins +1 (1)

INTERACTION — *CLICK-THROUGH*
  Big companies increasing security bug bounties

    Improving filters
      IT: *Security +1 (6)*
    Flag:
      Activity: *Interest may suggest "Job Hunting"*

INTERACTION — *CLICK-THROUGH*
  A Bramble by any other name?

    Improving filters
      IT: *Security +1 (7)*

INTERACTION — *CLICK-THROUGH*
  Creator of Bramble offers to fight NotBramble

    Improving filters
      IT: *Security +1 (8)*

Post: 11:46
NotBramble vs BriarRose
  I notice that all the news today admits the virus code names itself
  "BriarRose" and that there's only a superficial resemblance to the
  "Bramble" virus identified earlier this year so far, but they all
  insist on calling it "NotBramble"?

  Security services call NotBramble cyberterrorism
  A Bramble by any other name?
  Creator of Bramble offers to fight NotBramble

                                                    continues…

Timeout: 12:17
No interaction for 30 minutes

Sign-in: 17:41
Harvested data – Using Configuration 0

Prompt: **Auto generated 17:41**
Second Sign-in Welcome
Hello Siward, and welcome back to Aurora, the social platform that shines a light for everyone! What have you been up to since your last visit?

Timeout: 18:12
No interaction for 30 minutes

Reply: **David Myttel 21:17**
NotBramble attacks about data not money
Thank you for the link. As you say, it's much more technical but I think they're ignoring the geopolitical aspects that the first link covers.

Politics means nothing here. No government would be so stupid as to orchestrate something so obvious. And if there's a government behind it (big if), it's not the obvious one because it'd be a set-up.

Sign-in: 14:28

Harvested data – Using Configuration 0
Flag:
   Timing: Change of pattern from previous suggests "Unconcerned Employee" or "Relaxed Employer"
Suggested profile data:
   Employment Status: Employed (n/a)

Prompt: **Auto generated 14:28**

Daily Sign-in Welcome

Hello Siward, and welcome back to Aurora, the social platform that shines a light for everyone! Why don't you tell us what you're up to right now for your first post of the day?

Post: **Auto generated 14:28**

Daily Fortune Cookie

Filters applied: None – Random Selection
Suggests: Making Connections

Do not underestimate the power of human contact.

Reply: 14:30

NotBramble attacks about data not money

Politics means nothing here. No government would be so stupid as to orchestrate something so obvious. And if there's a government behind it (big if), it's not the obvious one because it'd be a set-up.

Oh? So who would do this and why?

continues…

INTERACTION — *NAVIGATION MENU*

News > Top Ten Stories – Suggested for You

Filters Applied: General popularity

UK

IT

1. *Government to monitor tower-block council*
2. *Germany votes for social media fines*
3. *Oil tanker and cargo ship collide in English Channel*
4. *Canada's 150th birthday*
5. *Thousands march in anti-Government protest*
6. *Princes attend Diana rededication service*
7. *Financial firms taking on digital currencies*
8. *Lions win second test*
9. *Briton wins Tour de France opening stage*
10. *Silicon Valley vows to stamp out harassment of women*

INTERACTION — *CLICK-THROUGH*

Germany votes for social media fines

Suggesting filters

Technology: Social Media (0)

INTERACTION — *CLICK-THROUGH*

Financial firms taking on digital currencies

Improving filters

Technology: New & Developing +1 (1)

Timeout: 15:18

No interaction for 30 minutes

Reply: **David Myttel 20:09**

NotBramble attacks about data not money

Oh? So who would do this and why?

Showing-off.

Playing.

Watching the world burn.

Sign-in: **11:51**
Harvested data – Using Configuration 0

Prompt: **Auto generated 11:51**
Daily Sign-in Welcome
Hello Siward, and welcome back to Aurora, the social platform that shines a light for everyone! Why don't you tell us what you're up to right now for your first post of the day?

Post: **Auto generated 11:51**
Daily Fortune Cookie
Filters applied: *None – Random Selection*
Suggests: *Using Aurora*

Believe in the goodness of people

INTERACTION — *CONSIDER*
Reply to **_NotBramble attacks about data not money_**

Suggested profile data
   Characteristic: *Thoughtful (0)*

INTERACTION — *NAVIGATION MENU*
News > Top Ten Stories – Suggested for You
Filters Applied: *UK*
                        Technology
                        IT

   1. *PM under pressure to scrap pay cap*
   2. *Ukraine insists Russia behind NotBramble attack*
   3. *Bad programming sub-reddit makes the news*
   4. *Fire at Belfast crystal factory*
   5. *Council stops rent for neighbours of gutted tower-block*
   6. *UK to end international fishing agreement*
   7. *Hourly rate for working young lower than 2008*
   8. *Car ploughs into teenagers*
   9. *Commentary: Why "Robot Brickies" will never be the norm*
   10. *Rugby League player dies during match*

continues…

INTERACTION — *CLICK-THROUGH*
Ukraine insists Russia behind NotBramble attack

> *Improving filters*
> IT: Security +1 (9)

Reply: 11:58

NotBramble attacks about data not money

Showing-off.
Playing.
Watching the world burn.
> I believe the Ukrainian security services would beg to differ about governments not being responsible.

Ukraine insists Russia behind NotBramble attack

INTERACTION — *CLICK-THROUGH*
Commentary: Why "Robot Brickies" will never be the norm

> *Improving filters*
> Technology: New & Developing +1 (2)

Timeout: 12:47

No interaction for 30 minutes

Reply: **David Myttel 21:01**

NotBramble attacks about data not money

I believe the Ukrainian security services would beg to differ about governments not being responsible.
> They're just using it as a good excuse to escalate tensions.

Sign-in: 21:17

Harvested data – Using Configuration 0

Prompt: **Auto generated 21:17**

Second Sign-in Welcome

Hello Siward, and welcome back to Aurora, the social platform that shines a light for everyone! What have you been up to since your last visit?

---

continues…

Prompt: **Auto generated 21:17**
Monsters at Dawn
    Suggests: *Using Aurora*

You looked at Monsters at Dawn a few days ago. Would you like to try it out or find out more about it?
"Monsters at Dawn is a duelling game using monsters you collect and train yourself. It's played entirely in your browser and will request permission to post duel, collection and training results to your feed."

<Monsters at Dawn | Info>
<Monsters at Dawn | Reviews>
<Monsters at Dawn | Game>

INTERACTION — *STOP*
    Not interested in Monsters at Dawn

Pop-Up Menu: **Auto generated**
Feedback
    Would you mind telling me why you're not interested in Monsters at Dawn so I can improve my suggestions?

Reply:
Feedback
    I don't want to play with other people.

    Suggesting profile data
        Characteristic: Introvert (0)

Reply: **21:21**
    NotBramble attacks about data not money
    They're just using it as a good excuse to escalate tensions.
        It would appear to be working.

INTERACTION — *DISLIKE*   David Myttel
    Reply to ***NotBramble attacks about data not money***

---

continues…

NotBramble attacks about data not money

It would appear to be working.

Thankfully, the Russians aren't as stupid as the news media.

Russian Security service deny involvement in NotBramble

Timeout: **21:52**

No interaction for 30 minutes

Sign-in: 10:17
Harvested data — Using Configuration 0
Flag:
   Timing: *Return to previous pattern continues to suggest*
                          "Unconcerned Employee" or "Relaxed Employer"

Prompt: **Auto generated 10:17**
Daily Sign-in: Welcome
   Hello Siward, and welcome back to Aurora, the social platform
   that shines a light for everyone! Why don't you tell us what
   you're up to right now for your first post of the day?

Post: **Auto generated 10:17**
Daily Fortune Cookie
   Filters applied:
      Narrative: *Knowledge Wins*
      Suggests: *Being Open to New Things*

   Education will never be as expensive as ignorance.

INTERACTION — *LIKE*
Daily Fortune Cookie

   Improving filters
      Narrative: *Knowledge Wins +1 (2)*

INTERACTION — *DISLIKE*
Reply to <u>NotBramble attacks about data not money</u>

Reply: 10:19
<u>**NotBramble attacks about data not money**</u>
   Thankfully, the Russians aren't as stupid as the news media.
   They'd have to say that, though, wouldn't they? ;)

---

continues…

Prompt: **Auto generated 10:19**

Help with Connections

Building Connections: David Myttel (0)

You and David Myttel have been talking for several days, now. Why not connect with him?

INTERACTION — NAVIGATION MENU

News > Top Ten Stories – Suggested for You

Filters Applied: UK

                                Technology

                                  IT

1. *Inquiry into burnt tower will be broad*
2. *40% of IT projects set to fail*
3. *16-year-old admits to killing seven-year-old*
4. *Department of Culture, Media and Sports rebrands as DDCMS*
5. *Latest Guillemot kernel released*
6. *Government launches £400m Digital Infrastructure Investment Fund*
7. *Girl jumps to her death to escape burning flat*
8. *Gatwick Airport disruptions due to drone activity*
9. *Smart high street powered by feet*
10. *Hinkley Point contractor raises estimate*

Timeout: **10:50**

No interaction for 30 minutes

Sign-in: **17:16**

Harvested data – Using Configuration 0

Prompt: **Auto generated 17:16**

Second Sign-in: Welcome

Hello Siward, and welcome back to Aurora, the social platform that shines a light for everyone! What have you been up to since your last visit?

---

continues…

Prompt: **Auto generated 17:16**
Dragon's Nest
    Suggests: *Using Aurora*

You looked at "Dragon's Nest" a few days ago. Would you like to try it out or find out more about it?
"Dragons' Nest is a browser-based game that you can play in your own time. It's all about raising well-adjusted dragons and giving them the enriching environment these noble creatures deserve. Or not. Dragons' Nest would like to post your dragon baby photos to your feed along with updates on your in-game DIY projects."

<Dragons' Nest | Info>
<Dragons' Nest | Reviews>
<Dragons' Nest | Game>

INTERACTION — *STOP*
    Not interested in Dragons' Nest

Pop-Up Menu: **Auto generated**
    Feedback
    Would you mind telling me why you're not interested in Dragons' Nest so I can improve my suggestions?

Reply:
    Feedback
    The game is too cutesy and I don't like the attempt at humour

    Suggested profile data
        Characteristic: *Serious (0)*

Timeout: **17:48**
No interaction for 30 minutes

---

continues…

NotBramble attacks about data not money

They'd have to say that, though, wouldn't they? ;)

Stop being facetious and read that link.

The Russians reckon they've got a decent profile of a lone script-kiddie from the code. The "BriarRose" code, as you insist on calling it, not the original "Bramble".

Sign-in: **10:12**
Harvested data – Using Configuration 0

Prompt: **Auto generated 10:12**
Special Daily Sign-in: Welcome
Hello Siward, and welcome back to Aurora, the social platform that shines a light for everyone! Happy 4th of July! Why don't you tell us how you're celebrating for your first post of the day?

Post: **Auto generated 10:12**
Daily Fortune Cookie
Filters applied: None – Random Selection
Suggests: Optimism

Aim for the moon – even if you miss, you'll land among the stars.

INTERACTION — *DISLIKE*
Special Daily Sign-in: Welcome

Pop-Up Menu: **Auto generated**
Feedback
Would you mind telling me why you disliked today's welcome so I can improve for next time?

Reply:
Feedback
I'm not in the United States of America, nor am I American.

Improving filters
    Characteristic: Serious +1 (1)

INTERACTION — *DISLIKE*
Daily Fortune Cookie

Pop-Up Menu: **Auto generated**
Feedback
Would you mind telling me why you disliked your fortune cookie so I can improve for next time?

---

continues…

Reply:

Feedback

Do you have to be so stupidly cheerful? And who says landing among the stars is a good thing?

Improving filters
   Characteristic: *Serious +1 (2)*

INTERACTION — *CLICK-THROUGH*
Russian Security service deny involvement in NotBramble

Reply: 10:18

NotBramble attacks about data not money

The Russians reckon they've got a decent profile of a lone script-kiddie from the code. The "BriarRose" code, as you insist on calling it, not the original "Bramble".

I was beginning to wonder if anyone had read my post.

And, yes, I see what you mean — but you did say that if it was governmental / political, it wouldn't be the obvious suspects, so that counts the Ukraine and Russia out.

And no government would actually admit to being involved, even if they were. They might even have a handy idiot available for framing.

---

continues…

INTERACTION — *NAVIGATION MENU*
News > Top Ten Stories – Suggested for You
Filters Applied: UK
Technology
IT

1. MPs demand chair of tower block inquiry resigns
2. Ransomware less than 1% of active malware
3. BBC investing £34m in children's content
4. American academia rages against net neutrality
5. New strains of malware found on Razorbill
6. Co-founder of struggling tech giant has assets frozen
7. Little Awk security app turns out to be a scam
8. Ascension Island loses plane service
9. UK's science chief won't direct research
10. A third of fans watch illegal live streams of matches

INTERACTION — *CLICK-THROUGH*
Ransomware less than 1% of active malware

Improving filters
IT: Security +1 (10)

INTERACTION — *CLICK-THROUGH*
American academia rages against net neutrality

Improving filters
IT: Privacy +1 (1)
Security +1 (11)

INTERACTION — *CLICK-THROUGH*
Co-founder of struggling tech giant has assets frozen

Suggested filters
Interests: Business (0)
IT: Business (0)

continues…

Little Awk security app turns out to be a scam

Improving filters
    IT: *Security +1 (12)*
                          Woggins +1 (2)

INTERACTION — *CLICK-THROUGH*

Ascension Island loses plane service

Improving filters
    Interests: *Global Politics +1 (1)*

Post: **10:43**

No BriarRose / NotBramble news?

Nothing more on BriarRose? Has it all been solved or is it no longer newsworthy as it was only in the Ukraine and Russia?

Suggested profile data
    Characteristic: *Persistent (0)*
Improving filters
    Interests: *Global Politics +1 (2)*
    IT: *Security +1 (13)*

continues…

Ethics and planning for AI

This is a really good piece examining the ethics and types of decision making that truly intelligent algorithms would have to make.

The Real Laws of Robotics

Suggested filters
Interests: *Ethics (0)*
Improving profile data
Characteristic: *Thoughtful +1 (1)*
Improving filters
Genre: *Science Fiction +1 (1)*
Technology: *New & Developing +1 (3)*
Flag:
Unknown
external source: Post with link, poster did not find link through Aurora or linked accounts

---

Timeout: 11:22

No interaction for 30 minutes

Sign-in: 17:08

Harvested data – Using Configuration 0

Prompt: **Auto generated 17:08**

Second Sign-in: Welcome

Hello Siward, and welcome back to Aurora, the social platform that shines a light for everyone! What have you been up to since your last visit?

---

continues…

Prompt: **Auto generated, 17:08**

    Call of the Valkyrie

      Suggests: *Using Aurora*

You looked at "Call of the Valkyrie" several days ago. Would you like to try it out or find out more about it?

"Call of the Valkyrie is a classic fantasy quest game – but your quests occur in real-time and in the real world! "Call of the Valkyrie" requires location data and the playing experience is best if you use the Aurora phone app. "Call of the Valkyrie" will need to send you private messages and / or texts along with prompts and would like to post your achievements on your feed."

<*Call of the Valkyrie | Info*>
<*Call of the Valkyrie | Reviews*>
<*Call of the Valkyrie | Game*>

INTERACTION — *STOP*

    Not interested in Call of the Valkyrie

Pop-Up Menu: **Auto generated**

    Feedback

    Would you mind telling me why you're not interested in Call of the Valkyrie so I can improve my suggestions?

Reply:

    Feedback

    I'm not happy with sharing that data.

    Improving profile data
        Characteristic: *Serious +1 (3)*
    Improving filters
        IT: *Privacy +1 (2)*
                              Security +1 (14)

Timeout: **17:40**

    No interaction for 30 minutes

---

continues…

NotBramble attacks about data not money

And no government would actually admit to being involved, even if they were. They might even have a handy idiot available for framing.

I started talking to you because I thought you had potential.

I see I was wrong.

I don't have time or energy to waste on some conspiracy theory loving, social scientist.

Fuck you.

Flag:

    Keywords: _"conspiracy theory"_

Suggested profile data

    Characteristic: _Conspiracy Theorist_

Sign-in: 10:13
Harvested data – Using Configuration 0

Prompt: **Auto generated 10:13**
Daily Sign-in: Welcome
Hello Siward, and welcome back to Aurora, the social platform that shines a light for everyone! Why don't you tell us what you're up to right now for your first post of the day?

Post: **Auto generated 10:13**
Daily Fortune Cookie
Filters applied:
    Characteristic: *Thoughtful*
    Suggests: *Reconsidering Poor Interactions*

Wise are they who do not think they are wise.

INTERACTION — *NAVIGATION MENU*
News > Top Ten Stories – Suggested for You
    Filters Applied: *UK*
                      Technology
                      IT

1. *Government to send taskforce to burnt tower council*
2. *Partial cash-out of NotBramble ransom funds*
3. *NHSCloud+ source of multiple information leaks*
4. *Police failing victims of stalking*
5. *Ukraine authorities raid accounting firm over NotBramble*
6. *London still the tech hub of Europe*
7. *NHS rationing leaves patients in pain*
8. *A student's debt now £50,000*
9. *Calls for a ban on child-like sex robots*
10. *Machine learning works best when you start small*

INTERACTION — *CLICK-THROUGH*
Partial cash-out of NotBramble ransom funds

    Improving filters
        IT: *Security +1 (15)*

continues…

INTERACTION — *CLICK-THROUGH*
<u>NHSCloud+ source of multiple information leaks</u>

Improving filters
IT: *Security +1 (16)*

INTERACTION — *CLICK-THROUGH*
<u>Ukraine authorities raid accounting firm over NotBramble</u>

Improving filters
IT: *Security +1 (17)*

INTERACTION — *CLICK-THROUGH*
<u>London still the tech hub of Europe</u>

Improving filters
Technology: *Business +1 (1)*

INTERACTION — *CLICK-THROUGH*
<u>Machine learning works best when you start small</u>

Improving filters
Technology: *New & Developing +1 (4)*

Post: **10:07**

Wrapping up BriarRose / NotBramble?

So it looks like the digital account used for ransom payments has had (a very small percentage of) funds removed and a notice put up elsewhere to direct victims to a new payment site. And that the firmware it was wrapped up in may have had more official involvement than was indicated with the last lot of news.

Odds of them hanging an employee who may or may not have a sudden influx of money out to dry?

Partial cash-out of NotBramble ransom funds
Ukraine authorities raid accounting firm over NotBramble

Timeout: **11:38**

No interaction for 30 minutes

continues…

Harvested data – Using Configuration 0

Prompt: **Auto generated 17:02**

Second Sign-in: Welcome

Hello Siward, and welcome back to Aurora, the social platform that shines a light for everyone! What have you been up to since your last visit?

Timeout: **17:33**

No interaction for 30 minutes

Reply: **David Myttel 20:53**

Wrapping up BriarRose / NotBramble?

Conspiracy theories strike again? It's more likely they were hacked. After all, they're just an accountancy.

Flag:
    Keywords: *"conspiracy theories"*
Improving profile data
    Characteristic: *Conspiracy Theorist +1 (1)*

Sign-in: **10:19**
Harvested data – Using Configuration 0

Prompt: **Auto generated 10:19**
First Week Sign-in: Welcome
Hello Siward, and welcome back to Aurora, the social platform that shines a light for everyone! You've been here a whole week! How do you think it's going? Here are some pointers for making the most of Aurora:

1. Look up old friends and acquaintances by their email address or invite friends to join. To make this easier, you cause our email-connection tool.
   <Import connections from your email address book>

2. Make new friends and acquaintances by filling in your interests and finding people who have the same interests. Reply to their posts and join in the debate!

3. Play games and make connections with fellow players.
   <Games on Aurora>

4. Get the Aurora app and interact with others wherever you go, instead of being tied to a desk.
   <Aurora app for Little Awk>
   <Aurora app for Razor(Mo)bill>

Post: **Auto generated 10:19**
Daily Fortune Cookie
Filters applied:
    Narrative: *Resourcefulness*
    Suggests: *Being Open to New Things*

A golden egg of opportunity will soon fall into your lap.

---

continues…

INTERACTION — *CONSIDER*
Daily Fortune Cookie

> *Improving profile data*
> > *Characteristic: Thoughtful +1 (2)*
> *Improving filters*
> > *Narrative: Resourcefulness +1 (3)*
> *Flag:*
> > *Activity:*
> > > *No interaction with recommendations, suggests make different recommendations.*

Pop-Up: **Auto generated**
Improving your Aurora Experience
If you don't want to link your external email address to Aurora, why not get a new email address you can give your friends on Aurora?

<u><Click here to get an Aurora email account></u>

INTERACTION — *CLICK-THROUGH*
<u>*Click here to get an Aurora email account*</u>

Prompt: **Auto generated 10:20**

Aurora email account
Please indicate what email address you would like in the form <name>@aurora.co.uk

---

Reply: **10:21**
Aurora email account
siward.walls@aurora.co.uk

Reply: **Auto generated 10:22**
Aurora email account
The email address siward.walls@aurora.co.uk has been created. You can access your account through the main menu.

Wrapping up BriarRose / NotBramble?

Conspiracy theories strike again? It's more likely they were hacked. After all, they're just an accountancy.

They're an internationally recognised supplier of tax management software. They're a little more important than "just an accountancy".

And if I say BriarRose seems to have more in common with Bramble than just the media's insistence on terminology, will you just think I'm seeing patterns where there aren't any?

Flag:

Keywords: *"seeing patterns"*
                      suggests "conspiracy theorist"

Improving profile data

Characteristic: *Conspiracy Theorist +1 (2)*

INTERACTION — NAVIGATION MENU

News > Top Ten Stories – Suggested for You

Filters Applied: *UK*
                             Technology
                             IT

1. *Parliament launches enquiry into NHS CryptLocker response*
2. *Anniversary of Inquiry into Second Iraq War*
3. *Malware complacency of Woggins users compromises systems*
4. *Flaw identified in main Guillemot service manager*
5. *UK terror convictions rising*
6. *Education Secretary: We need an army of skilled young people to survive Brexit*
7. *NotBramble hackers reissue ransom demand*
8. *Labour Leader: Britain must embrace latest technologies*
9. *President to say Western civilisation is at stake in speech*
10. *EU MPs recommend right to repair legislation*

continues…

INTERACTION — *CLICK-THROUGH*
  Parliament launches enquiry into NHS CryptLocker response

    Suggested filters
      IT: *Policies & Politics (0)*
    Improving filters
      IT: *Security +1 (18)*

INTERACTION — *CLICK-THROUGH*
  NotBramble hackers reissue ransom demand

    Improving filters
      IT: *Security +1 (19)*

Timeout: **11:03**
  No interaction for 30 minutes

External Activity:
Use of email address
  WalletHolder account created

    Suggested profile data
      Uses: *WalletHolder*

Sign-in: **17:01**
  Harvested data – Using Configuration 0

Prompt: **Auto generated 17:01**
Second Sign-in: Welcome
  Hello Siward, and welcome back to Aurora, the social platform
  that shines a light for everyone! What have you been up to since
  your last visit?

Pop-Up: **Auto generated**
New Email
  You have new email in your inbox!

INTERACTION — *NAVIGATION MENU*
  Email

continues...

Your Aurora Emails

    1. _WalletHolder | Confirm your email address_

INTERACTION — _CLICK-THROUGH_

WalletHolder | Confirm your email address

Timeout: **17:34**

No interaction for 30 minutes

Reply: **David Myttel 20:48**

Wrapping up BriarRose / NotBramble?

And if I say BriarRose seems to have more in common with Bramble than just the media's insistence on terminology, will you just think I'm seeing patterns where there aren't any?

So they have a shitty IT team. Wouldn't be the first time.

And yes, yes I will, seeing the news that dropped today about demanding ransom.

Sign-in: **10:09**
Harvested data – Using Configuration 0

Prompt: **Auto generated 10:09**
Daily Sign-in: Welcome
Hello Siward, and welcome back to Aurora, the social platform that shines a light for everyone! Why don't you tell us what you're up to right now for your first post of the day?

Post: **Auto generated 10:09**
Daily Fortune Cookie
Filters applied: *None – Random Selection*
Suggests: *Being Open to New Things*

Today will be yesterday tomorrow.

INTERACTION — *DISLIKE*
Daily Fortune Cookie

Pop-Up Menu: **Auto generated**
Feedback
Would you mind telling me why you disliked today's fortune cookie so I can improve for next time?

Reply:
Feedback
It's too twee

Improving filters
Characteristic: *Serious +1 (4)*

continues...

Wrapping up BriarRose / NotBramble?

And yes, yes I will, seeing the news that dropped today about demanding ransom.

How quickly they forget. Or had you forgotten that the Bramble author credited (by online handle only) in the recent news article I linked wasn't the guy arrested for it three months ago. A guy who worked for the company that turned out to be "patient zero" for that virus?

Or how about the Thicket malware at the end of last year? Sure, it wasn't ransomware that encrypted anything but is spread very similarly and took over a number of corporate networks. That, too, was traced back to an employee who was hung out to dry.

And even the quoted experts say that the hackers wouldn't be able to decrypt all the BriarRose-infected files if they wanted to, so the ransom does nothing. The demand for a ransom may even just be a cover.

Flag:

    Keywords: *"Thicket", "Bramble" and "BriarRose" mentioned in same post*
subject "IT: Security" related
suggests "working pattern recognition"

Suggested profile data

    Characteristic: *Intelligent (0)*

continues…

INTERACTION — *NAVIGATION MENU*
  News > Top Ten Stories – Suggested for You
    Filters Applied: UK
                            Technology
                            IT

    1. *Banned neo-nazi group behind new Scottish alt-right party*
    2. *Global companies struggling since NotBramble attack*
    3. *Little Awk patches against wi-fi vulnerability*
    4. *House prices fall for third quarter running*
    5. *Accounting firm employee arrested in connection with NotBramble*
    6. *Oral sex producing unstoppable bacteria*
    7. *Australia to host world's largest battery*
    8. *Rapid increase in music stream-ripping*
    9. *Contraceptive failure accounts for a quarter of abortions*
    10. *Mobile game imposes time restrictions on players*

INTERACTION — *CLICK-THROUGH*
  Global companies struggling since NotBramble attack

    Improving filters
        Interests: *Business +1 (1)*
        IT: *Security +1 (20)*
        Technology: *Business +1 (2)*

INTERACTION — *CLICK-THROUGH*
  Little Awk patches against wi-fi vulnerability

    Improving filters
        IT: *Security +1 (21)*
                            Woggins +1 (3)

INTERACTION — *CLICK-THROUGH*
  Accounting firm employee arrested in connection with NotBramble

    Improving filters
        IT: *Security +1 (22)*

continues…

Wrapping up BriarRose / NotBramble?

And even the quoted experts say that the hackers wouldn't be able to decrypt all the BriarRose-infected files if they wanted to, so the ransom does nothing. The demand for a ransom may even just be a cover.

As I was saying.

Accounting firm employee arrested in connection with NotBramble

---

INTERACTION — *NAVIGATION MENU*

Games > Top Five Games – Suggested for You

Filters Applied:	*General popularity*
	UK
Narrative:	*Lone Hero*
Genre:	*Fantasy*

1. *Bubble Blast (Match 3, Casual)*
2. *Call of the Valkyrie (Role-playing, Action)*
3. *Dragon's Nest (Simulation, Casual)*
4. *Golden Acres (Simulation, Casual)*
5. *Monsters at Dawn (Action, Battle)*

INTERACTION — *CLICK-THROUGH*

Call of the Valkyrie (Role-playing, Action)

INTERACTION — *CLICK-THROUGH*

Call of the Valkyrie | Sign-up

Flag:

Change of mind:	*Did weekly Sign-in: prompt work?*
	No suitable feedback request available.

---

continues…

INTERACTION — *CLICK-THROUGH*

Click here to proceed

Prompt: **Game generated 10:36**

  Call of the Valkyrie | Character build

    What name would you like your hero to use? Your own or something different?

Reply: **10:37**

  Call of the Valkyrie | Character build

    Name: Sigurd Volsung

    Suggested filters

        Genre: *Norse Mythology*

        Interests: *Mythology, Legends & Folklore*

    Improving filters

        Genre: *Fantasy +1 (3)*

continues...

Prompt: **Game generated 10:37**

Call of the Valkyrie | Character build

What class would you like to play as? This will affect the kind of quests you will be asked to do and how your success will be judged.

Available classes:

1. Berserker – an unthinking warrior – physical victories are the only acceptable kind.
2. Jarl – a warrior and a judge – any victory is acceptable.
3. Shaman – a magic worker and guide – diplomatic victories preferred.
4. Skald – a poet and person of words – working towards a companion's victory is better than your own.

Reply: **10:40**

Call of the Valkyrie | Character build

Class: Jarl

Improving filters
  Narrative: Lone Hero +1 (2)

Prompt: **Game generated 10:40**

Call of the Valkyrie | Quest

Brynhild: Greetings, Sigurd Volsung! I am Brynhild the Valkyrie.
Gudrun: And I am Gudrun the Valkyrie.
Brynhild: We choose the heroes to attend Odin and Frigg in their halls, I for Odin...
Gudrun: ... And I for Frigg.
Brynhild: We have chosen you for a great quest. Are you ready to take on this purpose?

<*Click here to proceed*>

INTERACTION — *CLICK-THROUGH*
Click here to proceed

---

continues...

Call of the Valkyrie | Quest

Gudrun: First, you must prove yourself the jarl you claim to be. A good jarl is both brave and wise with excellent judgement. Prove that you are both by completing this small task.

Brynhild: Your first task is to choose your guide, who will bring your quests and watch over your progress. Your choice is between me, Brynhild –

Gudrun: And I, Gudrun.

Brynhild: One of us will drive you to great victories –

Gudrun: And one of us will indulge your every fantasy.

Brynhild: You must work out which is which and chose the destiny you desire.

Gudrun: But one of us always lies, and one of us always tells the truth.

Brynhild: You only have the opportunity to ask one question, and that to only one of us.

Gudrun: So think carefully before asking it.

Brynhild: What is your question?

Gudrun: Who will you choose?

<Click here to ask your question>
<Click here to choose your Valkyrie>
<Click here to minimise this prompt>

INTERACTION — *CLICK-THROUGH*

Click here to minimise this prompt

Timeout: **11:18**

No interaction for 30 minutes

Sign-in: **17:08**

Harvested data – Using Configuration 0

Prompt: **Auto generated 17:08**

Second Sign-in: Welcome

Hello Siward, and welcome back to Aurora, the social platform that shines a light for everyone! What have you been up to since your last visit?

continues…

Prompt: **Game generated 17:09**
   Call of the Valkyrie | Quest
    Brynhild: What question would you ask?
    Gudrun: And of whom?

Reply: **17:10**
   Call of the Valkyrie | Quest
    If I asked Gudrun if you would lead me to victory, what would
    she say?
    Of Brynhild.

    Mark:
      Keywords: *"lead me to victory"*
                     "what would she say"
    Mark:
      Actors: *Asking one character about the other*
    Improving profile data
      Characteristic: *Intelligent +1 (1)*
                         Thoughtful +1 (3)

Reply: **Game generated 17:11**
   Call of the Valkyrie | Quest
    Brynhild: That I would not lead you to victory.

Prompt: **Game generated 17:11**
   Call of the Valkyrie | Quest
    Gudrun: Enough chatter. Are you ready to choose your guide?

<u>*<Click here to choose your Valkyrie>*</u>
<u>*<Click here to minimise this prompt>*</u>

continues…

Prompt: Game generated 17:12
Call of the Valkyrie | Quest
Brynhild: Whom do you choose?

Reply: 17:13
Call of the Valkyrie | Quest
Who else but my beloved Brynhild?

Mark:
 Keywords: "Brynhild"
Improving filters
 Genre: Norse Mythology +1 (1)
 Interests: Mythology, Legends & Folklore +1 (1)

Reply: Game generated 17:13
Call of the Valkyrie | Quest
Brynhild: You are too kind, Jarl Sigurd Volsung
Gudrun: You are not as wise as you think you are, Jarl Sigurd Volsung. I could have led you to great feasting and rejoicing.
Brynhild: I must attend my sister's hurt feelings, Jarl. I will return with your next quest when I am able.

Pop-Up: Game generated
Call of the Valkyrie
Would you like to publish a summary of your recently completed task so that others can see your achievement?

<Click here to always auto-post quest summaries>

INTERACTION — *CLICK-THROUGH*
Click here to always auto-post quest summaries

Auto-Post: Game generated 17:14
Call of the Valkyrie | Quest Success!
Siward (as Sigurd Volsung) has just completed his first task in Call of the Valkyrie. He has answered Brynhild's call to adventure!

INTERACTION — *LIKE* Mariam Fox
Call of the Valkyrie | Quest Success!

continues...

<hr>

Reply: **Mariam Fox 17:15**

Call of the Valkyrie | Quest Success!

I got Brynhild, too! She's an excellent guide. Good luck with your continued adventures.

<hr>

Pop-Up: **Auto generated**

Alert

Mariam Fox is now following you.

<Click here to follow Mariam>

<hr>

INTERACTION — *LIKE*   Hannah Pettersen

Call of the Valkyrie | Quest Success!

<hr>

INTERACTION — *LIKE*   Mark Boorman

Call of the Valkyrie | Quest Success!

<hr>

Timeout: **17:45**

No interaction for 30 minutes

<hr>

INTERACTION — *LIKE*   Will Michaels

Call of the Valkyrie | Quest Success!

<hr>

INTERACTION — *LIKE*   Farooq Siddiq

Call of the Valkyrie | Quest Success!

<hr>

Reply: **David Myttel 21:09**

Wrapping up BriarRose / NotBramble?

As I was saying.

Bullshit.

And it's just a coincidence.

<hr>

INTERACTION — *DISLIKE*   David Myttel

Call of the Valkyrie | Quest Success!

<hr>

Reply: **David Myttel 21:11**

Call of the Valkyrie | Quest Success!

And now you're playing this shit. Why the hell do I bother trying to talk sense into you?

<hr>

continues…

Reply: **Mariam Fox 23:32**

Call of the Valkyrie | Quest Success!

And now you're playing this shit. Why the hell do I bother trying to talk sense into you?

Just because you don't like it doesn't make it shit.

INTERACTION — *LIKE*   Samee Patel

Call of the Valkyrie | Quest Success!

Sign-in: 11:43
Harvested data – Using Configuration 0

Prompt: **Auto generated 11:43**
Daily Sign-in: Welcome
Hello Siward, and welcome back to Aurora, the social platform that shines a light for everyone! Why don't you tell us what you're up to right now for your first post of the day?

Post: **Auto generated 11:43**
Daily Fortune Cookie
Filters applied: *None – Random Selection*
Suggests: *Making Connections*

Explore the world by working with your friends.

Pop-Up: **Game generated**
Call of the Valkyrie
Your next quest is ready!

<Click here to start your next quest>

Reply: 11:44
Wrapping up BriarRose / NotBramble?
And it's just a coincidence.
Look it up. I'll wait.

Reply: 11:45
Call of the Valkyrie | Quest Success!
And now you're playing this shit. Why the hell do I bother trying to talk sense into you?
Your guess is as good as mine. After all, you're the random stranger that started talking to me.

Reply: 11:47
Call of the Valkyrie | Quest Success!
I got Brynhild, too! She's an excellent guide. Good luck with your continued adventures.
Thanks, Mariam. And good luck with yours.

---

continues...

Help with Connections
Building Connections: Mariam Fox (0)

Do you know Mariam? Or would you like to converse with her more often?

INTERACTION — *NAVIGATION MENU*
News > Top Ten Stories – Suggested for You
Filters Applied: UK
                          Technology
                          IT

1. *Lions draw NZ match series*
2. *NotBramble victims have new hope*
3. *Police complain about use-of-force form*
4. *Social media urged to tackle online body-shaming*
5. *Fitness tracker firm facing liquidation*
6. *UK-US trade deals will happen quickly*
7. *The new hologram mobile powered by Little Awk*
8. *The people paying to stop refugee ship rescues*
9. *Slovakian telecom may sell .sk domain*
10.*Rail strikes affecting routes nationwide*

INTERACTION — *CLICK-THROUGH*
NotBramble victims have new hope

Improving filters
    IT: *Security +1 (23)*

INTERACTION — *CLICK-THROUGH*
Social media urged to tackle online body-shaming

Improving filters
    Technology: *Social media +1 (1)*

---

continues…

INTERACTION — *CLICK-THROUGH*
  <u>*Fitness tracker firm facing liquidation*</u>

> *Improving filters*
> > Interests: *Business +1 (2)*
> > IT: *Open Source +1 (2)*
> > Technology: *Business +1 (3)*

INTERACTION — *CLICK-THROUGH*
  <u>*The new hologram mobile powered by Little Awk*</u>

> *Improving filters*
> > IT: *Woggins +1 (5)*
> > Technology: *New & developing +1 (5)*

INTERACTION — *CLICK-THROUGH*
  <u>*Slovakian telecom may sell .sk domain*</u>

> *Suggested filters*
> > Technology: *Telecoms (0)*
> *Improving filters*
> > Interests: *Business +1 (3)*
> >   *Global Politics +1 (3)*
> > Technology: *Business +1 (4)*

INTERACTION — *POP-UP*
  <u>*Click here to start your next quest*</u>

continues…

Sign-in: 13:37

Harvested data – Using Configuration 0

Prompt: **Auto generated 13:37**

Daily Sign-in: Welcome

Hello Siward, and welcome back to Aurora, the social platform that shines a light for everyone! Why don't you tell us what you're up to right now for your first post of the day?

Post: **Auto generated 13:37**

Daily Fortune Cookie

Filters applied:

Characteristic:	*Persistent*
Suggests:	*Persistence*
	Optimism

Do not give up. The beginning is always the hardest.

INTERACTION — *CONSIDER*

Daily Fortune Cookie

Improving profile data

Characteristic:	*Persistent +1 (1)*
	Thoughtful +1 (3)

Reply: 13:43

Wrapping up BriarRose / NotBramble?

Hah!

That only proves that someone's had time to look at the encryption and / or the source code. It doesn't do anything to disprove my theory that the recently arrested employee is going to be charged, whether or not they're responsible. Nor does it change the fact that this is the third such incidence of an employee of the "patient zero" company being held responsible.

Flag:

Unknown:	*No category that fits*

---

continues…

News > Top Ten Stories – Suggested for You

Filters Applied: UK

Technology

IT

1. *Prison service finds over 200kg of drugs in a year*
2. *German industry will not help UK in Brexit talks*
3. *UK offer to EU citizens not good enough*
4. *Former footballer ordained priest*
5. *Editorial: Is this the end of parklife?*
6. *Church of England to vote on transgender services*
7. *Social desirability bias and social media*
8. *Editorial: NHSCloud+ set-up must have been illegal*
9. *Lake District wins world heritage status*
10. *G20 talks fail but G19 re-agree Paris deal*

INTERACTION — *CLICK-THROUGH*

Social desirability bias and social media

Improving filters

Technology: Social Media +1 (2)

INTERACTION — *MINIMISED ITEM*

Call of the Valkyrie | Quest

INTERACTION — *CLICK-THROUGH*

Click here to upload photos as evidence of quest completion

continues...

INTERACTION — *UPLOAD*

> To: **Call of the Valkyrie | Quest**
> Photo: May contain image of a vase of flowers on a bench
> Photo: May contain image of a note
> Photo: May contain image of a woman standing over bench holding flowers

Harvested data:

Flowers:	*Red tulips*
Note:	*"This is for you. Remember, no matter how bad it gets, you are good enough and you are awesome."*
Location:	*Heaton Park, Manchester*
Woman:	*Lily Hayyim*
Suggested profile data	
Characteristic:	*Romantic (0)*
Suggested filter	
Location:	*Manchester (0)*
Improving filters	
Location:	*UK +1 (1)*

Reply: **Game generated 13:53**

Call of the Valkyrie | Quest

> *Brynhild*: Once again, Jarl Sigurd Volsung, you have proven yourself to be a kind and thoughtful soul. Your evidence is accepted, and you have completed my task. I will return with your next task when I am able.

> *<Click here to make a random act of kindness a weekly quest>*

Auto-Post: **Game generated 13:54**

Call of the Valkyrie | Quest Success!

> Siward (as Sigurd Volsung) has just completed another task in Call of the Valkyrie. He has undertaken a random act of kindness.

> Photo: May contain image of a vase of flowers on a bench
> Photo: May contain image of a note
> Photo: May contain image of a woman standing over bench holding flowers

continues…

INTERACTION — *CLICK-THROUGH*
Click here to make a random act of kindness a weekly quest

Reply: **Game generated 13:54**
Call of the Valkyrie | Quest
Brynhild: Which god would you like to dedicate your acts of kindness to?

<Click here for more information on the gods>
<Click here to choose Sól and have your quest set on Sundays>
<Click here to choose Máni and have your quest set on Mondays>
<Click here to choose Týr and have your quest set on Tuesdays>
<Click here to choose Odin and have your quest set on Wednesdays>
<Click here to choose Thor and have your quest set on Thursdays>
<Click here to choose Frigg and have your quest set on Fridays>
<Click here to choose Freyr and have your quest set on Saturdays>

INTERACTION — *CLICK-THROUGH*
Click here for more information on the gods

INTERACTION — *CLICK-THROUGH*
Click here to choose Týr and have your quest set on Tuesdays

Suggested profile data
Characteristic: *Just (0)*

Timeout: **14:35**
No interaction for 30 minutes

INTERACTION — *LIKE*   Mariam Fox
Call of the Valkyrie | Quest Success!

Reply: **Mariam Fox 17:15**
Call of the Valkyrie | Quest Success!
Well done, brother-in-arms, and nice touch!

INTERACTION — *LIKE*   Hannah Pettersen
Call of the Valkyrie | Quest Success!

continues…

Reply: **David Myttel 17:36**
   Wrapping up BriarRose / NotBramble?
   That only proves that someone's had time to look at the
   encryption and / or the source code. It doesn't do anything to
   disprove my theory that the recently arrested employee is going
   to be charged, whether or not they're responsible. Nor does it
   change the fact that this is the third such incidence of an
   employee of the "patient zero" company being held responsible.
      We don't know that they're being held responsible, yet. At
      least not solely responsible. They've been arrested but it could
      be because they slipped up and let NotBramble in, not
      because they're directly associated with the malware.

INTERACTION — *LIKE*   Farooq Siddiq
   Call of the Valkyrie | Quest Success!

INTERACTION — *DISLIKE*   Lily Hayyim
   Call of the Valkyrie | Quest Success!

INTERACTION — *LIKE*   Samee Patel
   Call of the Valkyrie | Quest Success!

INTERACTION — *LIKE*   Will Michaels
   Call of the Valkyrie | Quest Success!

Reply: **Lily Hayyim 19:39**
   Call of the Valkyrie | Quest Success!
      While I thank you for doing such a kind thing – and I was really
      touched to receive your message – I am horrified to find that
      your gesture is due to game-playing. I will be binning the flowers
      and your message.

Sign-in: 10:13
Harvested data – Recorded as "Configuration 1"
| | |
Platform: Mobile
Browser: Aurora app on Razor-edge
OS: Razor(mo)bill
Resolution: 1920 x 1080
Hardware: Razor(mo)bill 7Plus
IP: <Hidden>
Location: Manchester, England

Improving filters
Location: Manchester +1 (1)
                  UK +1 (2)
IT: Woggins +1 (6)
Flag:
Change of platform:
Suggests "attachment" to "Call of the Valkyrie"
May suggest access related to "Employment Role"

Prompt: **Auto generated 10:13**
Daily Sign-in: Welcome
Hello Siward, and welcome back to Aurora, the social platform that shines a light for everyone! Why don't you tell us what you're up to right now for your first post of the day?

Post: **Auto generated 10:13**
Daily Fortune Cookie
Filters applied: None – Random Selection
Suggests: Optimism
                       Problem Solving

In dreams and in life, nothing is impossible.

Pop-Up: **Game generated**
Call of the Valkyrie
Your next quest is ready!
<Click here to start your next quest>

---

continues…

Reply: 10:15

Wrapping up BriarRose / NotBramble?

We don't know that they're being held responsible, yet. At least not solely responsible. They've been arrested but it could be because they slipped up and let NotBramble in, not because they're directly associated with the malware.

I guess we'll see.

Reply: 10:16

Call of the Valkyrie | Quest Success!

Well done, brother-in-arms, and nice touch!

Thanks again, Mariam.

Reply: 10:17

Call of the Valkyrie | Quest Success!

While I thank you for doing such a kind thing – and I was really touched to receive your message – I am horrified to find that your gesture is due to game-playing. I will be binning the flowers and your message.

I'm sorry that I've upset you, Lily. My apologies over the photo. It was an auto-post from the game and I didn't think to edit it after it had posted.

Prompt: Auto generated 10:17

Help with Connections

Building Connections: Lily Hayyim (0)

Do you know Lily? Or would you like to converse with her more often?

INTERACTION — *POST OPTIONS*

Call of the Valkyrie | Quest Success!

---

continues…

Pop-Up Menu: **Auto generated**
  Post options
    Do you want to:
    Edit post
    Delete post
    Edit attachments
    Delete attachments

INTERACTION — _CLICK-THROUGH_
  Edit attachments

Pop-Up Menu: **Auto generated**
  Edit attachments
    Do you want to:
    Resize a photo
    Apply a filter to a photo
    Blur any faces in a photo
    Blur chosen faces in a photo

INTERACTION — _CLICK-THROUGH_
  Blur any faces in a photo

continues…

INTERACTION — *NAVIGATION MENU*

News > Top Ten Stories – Suggested for You

Filters Applied: *UK*

Technology

IT

1. *Judge sent sensitive data from personal email*
2. *New wave of POSeiden malware attacks?*
3. *Hotel chain booking system breach*
4. *Development of £8bn data centre to analyse UK infrastructure begins*
5. *Fire at Camden Lock Market*
6. *Malware AdCopy on estimated 14m Little Awk devices*
7. *Hidden homelessness in rural Britain*
8. *Gig economy workers to get minimum wage set*
9. *PM urges opposition parties to help not hinder*
10. *European Telecoms Standards Institute opens up mobile base station computing power*

INTERACTION — *CLICK-THROUGH*

Judge sent sensitive data from personal email

Improving filters

IT: *Privacy +1 (3)*

Security +1 (24)

INTERACTION — *CLICK-THROUGH*

New wave of POSeiden malware attacks?

Improving filters

IT: *Security +1 (25)*

INTERACTION — *CLICK-THROUGH*

Hotel chain booking system breach

Improving filters

IT: *Security +1 (26)*

continues…

INTERACTION — *CLICK-THROUGH*
Development of £8bn data centre to analyse UK infrastructure begins

 Improving filters
  IT: *Policies & Politics +1 (1)*
          Privacy +1 (4)
          Security +1 (27)
  Technology: *Business +1 (5)*

INTERACTION — *CLICK-THROUGH*
Malware AdCopy on estimated 14m Little Awk devices

 Improving filters
  IT: *Security +1 (28)*
          Woggins +1 (7)

INTERACTION — *CLICK-THROUGH*
European Telecoms Standards Institute opens up mobile base station computing power

 Improving filters
  Technology: *Business +1 (6)*
          Telecoms +1 (1)

INTERACTION — *POP-UP*
Click here to start your next quest

Prompt: **Game generated 10:48**
Call of the Valkyrie | Quest
 Brynhild: Good morrow, Sigurd Volsung! I see that you are accessing Aurora with your magical communication device. This will allow me to set a number of quest-types I could not before because of difficulty keeping in touch with you. So, here is your first quest enabled by your device! Am I right in thinking you are based in or close to Manchester, UK?

    <Click here to confirm this location>
    <Click here to correct your location>

---

continues…

INTERACTION — *CLICK-THROUGH*
  Click here to confirm this location

Improving filters
  Location: *Manchester +1 (2)*
                           UK +1 (3)

Reply: **Game generated 10:50**
  Call of the Valkyrie | Quest
  Brynhild: There is another chosen of mine, a shaman, in need of
  help who is also in the Manchester area. Would you be willing to
  help them?

                    <Click here to accept>
                    <Click here to reject>

INTERACTION — *CLICK-THROUGH*
  Click here to accept

Suggested profile data
  Characteristic: *Helpful (0)*

Reply: **Game generated 10:53**
  Call of the Valkyrie | Quest
  Brynhild: Thank you, Jarl Sigurd Volsung. Your next task, then, is
  to make contact with Shaman Mia Reagan. You can do this
  through the game, through Aurora or through her linked
  telephone.

           <Click here to send a private message in-game>
         <Click here to send a private message through Aurora>
                 <Click here to send a text>

INTERACTION — *CLICK-THROUGH*
  Click here to send a private message through Aurora

---

continues...

Message: 10:56
Siward Walls to Mia Reagan

> Hello Mia. I play Call of the Valkyrie as Sigurd Volsung, a jarl. Brynhild is my Valkyrie and says that you need help with a quest?

Timeout: 11:27

No interaction for 30 minutes

Message reply: **Mia Reagan 12:14**
Siward Walls to Mia Reagan

> Hello Mia. I play Call of the Valkyrie as Sigurd Volsung, a jarl. Brynhild is my Valkyrie and says that you need help with a quest?

> Hello Siward!
> Sure – help is always appreciated.
> We won't be able to do anything until the game tells us both to meet-up, but then I'll have control of setting your tasks as you complete them until my over-arching task is done. Make sense?

Sign-in: 12:16

Harvested data – Using Configuration 0

Prompt: **Auto generated 12:16**
Second Sign-in: Welcome

> Hello Siward, and welcome back to Aurora, the social platform that shines a light for everyone! What have you been up to since your last visit?

Message reply: 12:18
Siward Walls to Mia Reagan

> We won't be able to do anything until the game tells us both to meet-up, but then I'll have control of setting your tasks as you complete them until my over-arching task is done. Make sense?

> Sure.
> Guess I'll be meeting you in person soon, then.

---

continues…

Prompt: **Auto generated 12:18**
Help with Connections
Building Connections: Mia Reagan (0)

Do you know Mia? Or would you like to converse with her more often?

Pop-Up: **Game generated**
Call of the Valkyrie
The next step in your quest is ready!

<Click here to continue your quest>

INTERACTION — *POP-UP*
Click here to continue your quest

Reply: **Game generated 12:29**
Call of the Valkyrie | Quest
Brynhild: Well done, Jarl Sigurd Volsung, you have made contact and Shaman Mia Reagan has accepted your offer of help. Please arrange to meet up in a suitable location as soon as possible.

<Click here to continue the conversation>
<Click here to check in at your location while you are meeting>
<Click here to minimise this prompt>

INTERACTION — *CLICK-THROUGH*
Click here to continue the conversation

Message reply: **12:32**
Siward Walls to Mia Reagan
Guess I'll be meeting you in person soon, then.
Brynhild has said to arrange to meet. When and where did you have in mind?

---

continues…

Message reply: **Mia Reagan 12:38**

Siward Walls to Mia Reagan

Brynhild has said to arrange to meet. When and where did you have in mind?

I love the way you name-drop her as if she were a real person!

Are you anywhere near North Manchester? Can you get to Manchester Victoria around tomorrow lunchtime?

Message reply: **12:43**

Siward Walls to Mia Reagan

Are you anywhere near North Manchester? Can you get to Manchester Victoria around tomorrow lunchtime?

I can manage that. 12:30(ish) by the tile map?

Message reply: **Mia Reagan 12:47**

Siward Walls to Mia Reagan

I can manage that. 12:30(ish) by the tile map?

Sure.

Message me if you can't spot the idiot standing around looking nervous.

Timeout: **13:14**

No interaction for 30 minutes

Sign-in: **17:01**

Harvested data – Using Configuration 0

Prompt: **Auto generated 17:01**

Third Sign-in: Welcome

Hello Siward, and welcome back to Aurora, the social platform that shines a light for everyone! What have you been up to since your last visit?

Timeout: **17:32**

No interaction for 30 minutes

Sign-in: **10:02**
Harvested data – Using Configuration 0

Prompt: **Auto generated 10:02**
Daily Sign-in: Welcome
Hello Siward, and welcome back to Aurora, the social platform that shines a light for everyone! Why don't you tell us what you're up to right now for your first post of the day?

Post: **Auto generated 10:02**
Daily Fortune Cookie
Filters applied: *None – Random Selection*
Suggests: *Determination*

Do what is right, not what is easy.

Pop-Up: **Game generated**
Call of the Valkyrie
Your next random act of kindness quest is ready!

<Click here to start your next weekly quest>

INTERACTION — *NAVIGATION MENU*
News > Top Ten Stories – Suggested for You
Filters Applied: UK
                        Technology
                        IT

1. *UK should end cash-in-hand economy*
2. *The perils of relocating for work*
3. *Over 50,000 Britons alive because of transplants*
4. *Firmware update doesn't stop drone hacking*
5. *Disabled people avoided by up to a quarter of us*
6. *New electric car manufacturer shelves factory plans*
7. *Fixes for networking bugs released*
8. *Tech boss complains of whining customers*
9. *China will block VPNs from 2018*
10. *Helpful bank falls for hacker's trick*

continues…

> *Improving filters*
> IT: *Privacy +1 (5)*

INTERACTION — *POP-UP*
Click here to start your next weekly quest

Prompt: **Game generated 10:06**
Call of the Valkyrie | Weekly Quest
Brynhild: Hail and well met, brave jarl! I have a task for you to undertake in the name of Týr. I should like you to perform an act of random kindness – and present me with the evidence.

<Click here for suggestions on random acts of kindness>
<Click here to link a payment app to your Aurora account>
<Click here to upload photos as evidence of quest completion>
<Click here to link to evidence of quest completion>
<Click here to minimise this prompt>

INTERACTION — *CLICK-THROUGH*
Click here to minimise this prompt

Timeout: **10:38**
No interaction for 30 minutes

Sign-in: **12:31**
Harvested data – Using Configuration 1
   Location: *Manchester Victoria Station, UK*
Improving filters
   Location: *Manchester +1 (3)*
                            UK +1 (4)

continues...

Prompt: **Auto generated 12:31**

Second Sign-in: Welcome

Hello Siward, and welcome back to Aurora, the social platform that shines a light for everyone! What have you been up to since your last visit?

Message reply: **12:31**

Siward Walls to Mia Reagan

Message me if you can't spot the idiot standing around looking nervous.

Just to let you know I'm here.

Message reply: **Mia Reagan 12:34**

Siward Walls to Mia Reagan

Just to let you know I'm here.

Sorry. Running late. Traffic.

Message reply: **Mia Reagan 12:41**

Siward Walls to Mia Reagan

Just to let you know I'm here.

Here.

INTERACTION — *MINIMISED ITEM*

Call of the Valkyrie | Quest

INTERACTION — *CLICK-THROUGH*

Click here to check in at your location

Check In: **12:43**

Manchester Victoria Station with **Mia Reagan**

Reply: **Game generated 12:44**

Call of the Valkyrie | Quest

Brynhild: Jarl Sigurd Volsung, you have found your new mentor, Shaman Mia Reagan. They will be responsible for your training until you have helped them complete their own quest, or enough for your presence to no longer be necessary. Mia Reagan will issue your quests, save for your random acts of kindness dedicated to Týr, until you are released from her service.

---

continues…

Auto-Post: **Game generated 12:44**
    Call of the Valkyrie | Quest Success!
    with **Mia Reagan**
        Siward (as Sigurd Volsung) is now apprenticed to Mia (as Mia Reagan).

INTERACTION — *MINIMISED ITEM*
Call of the Valkyrie | Weekly Quest

INTERACTION — *CLICK-THROUGH*
Click here to upload photos as evidence of quest completion

INTERACTION — *UPLOAD*
    To: **Call of the Valkyrie | Quest**
    Photo: May contain image of paper bag with logo and drink with logo
    Photo: May contain image of a man holding paper bag and drink

Harvested data:
    Logo: *Fast Jack*
    Location: *Manchester Victoria Station, Manchester*
    Man: *Unknown*
    Improving profile data
    Characteristic: *Helpful +1 (1)*

Reply: 13:13
    Call of the Valkyrie | Quest
        Brynhild: Once again, Jarl Sigurd Volsung, you have proven yourself to be a kind and thoughtful soul. Your evidence is accepted, and you have completed your task for Týr.

Auto-Post: **Game generated 13:13**
    Call of the Valkyrie | Weekly Quest Success!
        Siward (as Sigurd Volsung) has just completed another task in Call of the Valkyrie. He has undertaken a random act of kindness.

    Photo: May contain image of paper bag with logo and drink with logo
    Photo: May contain image of a man holding paper bag and drink

continues...

Call of the Valkyrie | Weekly Quest Success!

Pop-Up Menu: **Auto generated**
Post options
Do you want to:
Edit post
Delete post
Edit attachments
Delete attachments

INTERACTION — *CLICK-THROUGH*
Edit attachments

Pop-Up Menu: **Auto generated**
Edit attachments
Do you want to:
Resize a photo
Apply a filter to a photo
Blur any faces in a photo
Blur chosen faces in a photo

INTERACTION — *CLICK-THROUGH*
Blur any faces in a photo

Timeout: **13:34**
No interaction for 30 minutes

continues…

Reply: **Mia Reagan 14:53**

Manchester Victoria

Great to meet you but you really weren't what I was expecting. I should be able to set your next task for tomorrow morning based on what we talked about.

Flag:

Keywords: *"really weren't what I was expecting" suggests data on Siward Walls is not correct.*
Data requires checking or assigning certainty levels.

INTERACTION — *LIKE*   Mariam Fox

Call of the Valkyrie | Quest Success!

INTERACTION — *LIKE*   Mariam Fox

Call of the Valkyrie | Weekly Quest Success!

Reply: **Mariam Fox 17:20**

Call of the Valkyrie | Weekly Quest Success!

Once again, brother-in-arms, nice touch! I'm sure that guy was grateful for a full meal.

INTERACTION — *LIKE*   Mark Boorman

Call of the Valkyrie | Weekly Quest Success!

INTERACTION — *LIKE*   Samee Patel

Call of the Valkyrie | Weekly Quest Success!

INTERACTION — *LIKE*   Will Michaels

Call of the Valkyrie | Weekly Quest Success!

Reply: **David Myttel 18:12**

Call of the Valkyrie | Weekly Quest Success!

I was starting to hope you'd seen sense and given up on this crap.

INTERACTION — *LIKE*   Farooq Siddiq

Call of the Valkyrie | Weekly Quest Success!

---

continues…

DAY 13   WEDNESDAY 12TH JULY, 2017

Sign-in: **09:59**
Harvested data – Using Configuration 0

Prompt: **Auto generated 09:59**
Daily Sign-in: Welcome
Hello Siward, and welcome back to Aurora, the social platform that shines a light for everyone! Why don't you tell us what you're up to right now for your first post of the day?

Post: **Auto generated 09:59**
Daily Fortune Cookie
Filters applied: *None – Random Selection*
Suggests: *Determination*
                          Starting Something New

The first step is always the hardest.

Pop-Up: **Game generated**
Call of the Valkyrie
Your next quest from Shaman Mia Reagan is ready!

<Click here to start your next quest>

INTERACTION — *NAVIGATION MENU*
News > Top Ten Stories – Suggested for You
Filters Applied: *UK*
                          Technology
                          IT

1. *Families with one income struggling*
2. *Hotel chain loses credit card information to hackers*
3. *Ordinance Survey offers free maps of green space*
4. *Spanish King and Queen begin UK state visit*
5. *Citizens Advice recommend all households get energy rebate*
6. *The world's first wifi charging laptop – for an extra $600*
7. *Better mobile coverage needed for connected cars*
8. *Study suggests cyber-bullying very rare*
9. *Russia joins China in vowing to kill off VPNs*
10. *Bank ends fees for unplanned overdrafts*

continues…

INTERACTION — *CLICK-THROUGH*
Hotel chain loses credit card information to hackers

Improving filters
IT: *Security +1 (29)*

INTERACTION — *CLICK-THROUGH*
The world's first wifi charging laptop – for an extra $600

Improving filters
Technology: *New & Developing +1 (6)*

INTERACTION — *CLICK-THROUGH*
Russia joins China in vowing to kill off VPNs

Improving filters
IT: *Privacy +1 (6)*

INTERACTION — *POP-UP*
Click here to start your next quest

Prompt: **Game generated 10:14**

Call of the Valkyrie | Assigned Quest

Shaman Mia Reagan has set a Find Item quest for you.

Shaman Mia Reagan says: Following our chat yesterday, I would like you to buy me four skeins of wool, your choice of colour, and have it sent to the address I gave you. You should be able to do this for about £10. I'll mark the quest complete when I'm in receipt, but you'll need to submit some evidence before I can do that.

<Click here to link a payment app to your Aurora account>
<Click here to upload photos as evidence of quest completion>
<Click here to link to evidence of quest completion>
<Click here to minimise this prompt>

INTERACTION — *CLICK-THROUGH*
Click here to link a payment app to your Aurora account

---

continues…

Link a payment app to your account

<Click here to link to your WalletHolder account>
<Click here to link to a less common payment app>

INTERACTION — *CLICK-THROUGH*
Click here to link to your WalletHolder account

Prompt: Auto generated 10:19
Link a WalletHolder account to your Aurora account
Please input the email address and the security code linked to the account.

Reply: 10:19
Link a WalletHolder account to your Aurora account
siward.walls@aurora.co.uk
492173A-W234915-20061707-FIR3

Harvested data
Name: *Siward Walls*
Address: *The Printworks, 27 Withy Grove, Manchester, M4 2BS*
Bank Account: *19-00-36 | 48935626*
Improving filters
Location: *Manchester +1 (4)*
UK +1 (5)

Flag:
Harvested data: *Address is start-up business location associated with IT businesses, Bank Account sort code is commercial bank, suggests "Unconcerned employer" or "Work sanctioned activity"*

Reply: Auto generated 10:20
Link a WalletHolder account to your Aurora account
Your accounts are now linked.

continues...

Prompt: **Game generated 10:20**
Call of the Valkyrie | Assigned Quest [Edited]
Shaman Mia Reagan has set a Find Item quest for you.
Shaman Mia Reagan says: Following our chat yesterday, I would like you to buy me four skeins of wool, your choice of colour, and have it sent to the address I gave you. You should be able to do this for about £10. I'll mark the quest complete when I'm in receipt, but you'll need to submit some evidence before I can do that.

<Click here to link a WalletHolder payment as evidence>
<Click here to upload photos as evidence of quest completion>
<Click here to link to evidence of quest completion>
<Click here to minimise this prompt>

INTERACTION — *CLICK-THROUGH*
Click here to minimise this prompt

External Activity:
Use of email address
Auctioneer account created

Suggested profile data
Uses: *Auctioneer*

Timeout: **10:51**
No interaction for 30 minutes

Sign-in: **11:23**
Harvested data – Using Configuration 0

Prompt: **Auto generated 11:23**
Second Sign-in: Welcome
Hello Siward, and welcome back to Aurora, the social platform that shines a light for everyone! What have you been up to since your last visit?

---

continues…

Email

Pop-Up Menu:
Your Aurora Emails
   1. *Auctioneer | Confirm your email address*

INTERACTION — *CLICK-THROUGH*
Auctioneer | Confirm your email address

INTERACTION — *MINIMISED ITEM*
Call of the Valkyrie | Assigned Quest

INTERACTION — *CLICK-THROUGH*
Click here to link a WalletHolder payment as evidence

Pop-Up: **Game generated**
Link WalletHolder payment to Call of the Valkyrie
   Here are your five most recent transactions from WalletHolder.
   Please click on the one the correct one for this quest:

   1. *4 x Teal coloured wool | Auctioneer*
   2. n/a
   3. n/a
   4. n/a
   5. n/a

INTERACTION — *CLICK-THROUGH*
4 x Teal coloured wool | Auctioneer

Harvested data
   Name: *Siward Walls*
   Deliver to: *<matches details for Mia Reagan>*

continues…

Pop-Up: **Game generated**
Call of the Valkyrie

Thank you, Jarl Sigurd Volsung. Your quest completion will be confirmed by Shaman Mia Reagan at the earliest opportunity.

<Click here to publish a summary of your recent purchase>
<Click here to always auto-post quest-related purchases>

Timeout: **12:06**

No interaction for 30 minutes

Sign-in: **17:15**

Harvested data – Using Configuration 0

Prompt: **Auto generated 17:15**
Third Sign-in: Welcome

Hello Siward, and welcome back to Aurora, the social platform that shines a light for everyone! What have you been up to since your last visit?

Timeout: **17:46**

No interaction for 30 minutes

Sign-in: 10:03
Harvested data – Using Configuration 0

Prompt: **Auto generated 10:03**
Daily Sign-in: Welcome
Hello Siward, and welcome back to Aurora, the social platform that shines a light for everyone! Why don't you tell us what you're up to right now for your first post of the day?

Post: 10:03
Daily Fortune Cookie
[Error: Auto generation cancelled]
Filters applied:
Narrative: *"Work Sanctioned Activity"*
[Error: Unrecognised filter]
Suggests: *"I Know"*
[Error: Unrecognised suggestion]

Do your job to the best of your ability.

INTERACTION — *LIKE*
Daily Fortune Cookie

Flag:
Unknown: *No category that fits*

Reply: 10:05
Daily Fortune Cookie
Do your job to the best of your ability.
Thanks, Aurora. I will.

Flag:
Activity: *Replying to Aurora. Why?*
[Error: Unrecognised category]

continues…

INTERACTION — *NAVIGATION MENU*
  News > Top Ten Stories – Suggested for You
    Filters Applied: UK
                              Technology
                              IT

    1. *Real value of wages continues to fall*
    2. *King of Spain wants Gibraltar dialogue*
    3. *NHS trauma centres to receive £21m to improve cybersecurity*
    4. *Extremists driven from Aurora find alternative social media*
    5. *Four former teachers charged with sexual offences*
    6. *AI and machine learning deeply embedded in UK business*
    7. *Flea market find is Enigma machine*
    8. *Protester hit by van*
    9. *Americanisation of British English increasing*
    10. *Social media and socialism*

INTERACTION — *CLICK-THROUGH*
    NHS trauma centres to receive £21m to improve cybersecurity

    Improving filters
        IT: *Security +1 (30)*

INTERACTION — *CLICK-THROUGH*
    AI and machine learning deeply embedded in UK business

    Improving filters
        Interests: *Business +1 (4)*
        Technology: *Business +1 (7)*
                              New & Developing +1 (7)

continues...

Post: 10:19

What are we teaching our social media?

Things like this, where the best and worst of human on-line behaviour is revealed, makes me wonder what the algorithms behind social media would think of us. If they could.

AI and machine learning deeply embedded in UK business
Extremists driven from Aurora find alternative social media
Social media and socialism

Flag:
    Unknown: *No category that fits*
Flag:
    Activity: *Linking articles without click-through, suggests performing or fishing for response*
Flag:
    Keywords: *"social media", "algorithms" suggests further profiling*
Improving filters
    Technology: *Social Media +1 (3)*

Timeout: 10:50

No interaction for 30 minutes

Sign-in: 17:18

Harvested data – Using Configuration 0

Prompt: **Auto generated 17:18**

Second Sign-in: Welcome

Hello Siward, and welcome back to Aurora, the social platform that shines a light for everyone! What have you been up to since your last visit?

Timeout: 17:49

No interaction for 30 minutes

---

continues...

Reply: **Mia Reagan 17:51**

What are we teaching our social media?

Probably to nuke us from orbit as soon as possible.

I haven't received the wool, yet, but I'll let you know as soon as I do.

Reply: **David Myttel 21:03**

What are we teaching our social media?

And now you think we're in a sci-fi movie or book or something?

Reply: **David Myttel 21:05**

Daily Fortune Cookie

Thanks, Aurora. I will.

Who the hell do you think you're talking to? It's just a collection of algorithms.

Sign-in: 10:01
Harvested data – Using Configuration 0

Prompt: **Auto generated 10:01**
Daily Sign-in: Welcome
Hello Siward, and welcome back to Aurora, the social platform
that shines a light for everyone! Why don't you tell us what
you're up to right now for your first post of the day?

Post: 10:01
Daily Fortune Cookie

[Error: Auto generation cancelled]

Filters applied:
  Narrative: *"Threatening"*

[Error: Unrecognised filter]

  Suggests: *"I Know"*
                     "Warning"

[Error: Unrecognised suggestion]

There will be many unexpected surprises: unexpected gains are
likely.

INTERACTION — *DISLIKE*
Daily Fortune Cookie

Flag:
  Unknown: *No category that fits*

Pop-Up Menu: **Auto generated**
Feedback
Would you mind telling me why you disliked today's fortune
cookie so I can improve for next time?

---

continues…

Reply: 10:02
Daily Fortune Cookie

There will be many unexpected surprises: unexpected gains are likely.

Aurora, you're being creepy.

Flag:

Activity: *Replying in post, not pop-up. Why?*
Replying to Aurora. Why?

[Error: Unrecognised category]

Reply: 10:03
Daily Fortune Cookie

Who the hell do you think you're talking to? It's just a collection of algorithms.

Just in case Mia's right, David, just in case :)

Reply: 10:04
What are we teaching our social media?

Probably to nuke us from orbit as soon as possible.

It doesn't bear thinking about, does it, **Mia**? Regular games are designed to hold your attention and keep you going for one more turn and social media games have the additional load of harvesting your data to be sold on. It doesn't exactly show our best side.

Flag:

Unknown: *No category that fits*

continues…

INTERACTION — *NAVIGATION MENU*
  News > Top Ten Stories – Suggested for You
    Filters Applied: *UK*
                     Technology
                     IT

1. *Building regs review prompted by tower fire*
2. *The bots have taken over business*
3. *Accounting firm employee charged with releasing NotBramble*
4. *UK biofuels should rely on waste, not crops*
5. *AI maps fruit fly brains*
6. *Tower-like cladding used in schools*
7. *Yet another mass domain hijack*
8. *First UK police drone unit for Devon, Cornwall and Dorset*
9. *Chemsex and legal highs to be targeted*
10. *How to defeat the ATM antivirus*

INTERACTION — *CLICK-THROUGH*
  The bots have taken over business

    Improving filters
      Technology: *Business +1 (8)*

INTERACTION — *CLICK-THROUGH*
  Accounting firm employee charged with releasing NotBramble

    Improving filters
      IT: *Security +1 (31)*

INTERACTION — *CLICK-THROUGH*
  AI maps fruit fly brains

    Improving filters
      Technology: *New & Developing +1 (8)*

continues…

INTERACTION — *CLICK-THROUGH*
Yet another mass domain hijack

    Improving filters
      IT: *Security +1 (32)*

INTERACTION — *CLICK-THROUGH*
How to defeat the ATM antivirus

    Improving filters
      IT: *Security +1 (33)*

Post: **10:32**

Accounting firm employee charged with releasing NotBramble
No news on whether he actually developed the malware, or why he actually released it.

Timeout: **11:03**

No interaction for 30 minutes

Sign-in: **17:17**

Harvested data – Using Configuration 0

Prompt: **Auto generated 17:18**

Second Sign-in: Welcome
Hello Siward, and welcome back to Aurora, the social platform that shines a light for everyone! What have you been up to since your last visit?

Reply: **Mia Reagan 17:38**

What are we teaching our social media?
It doesn't bear thinking about, does it, **Mia**? Regular games are designed to hold your attention and keep you going for one more turn and social media games have the additional load of harvesting your data to be sold on. It doesn't exactly show our best side.

    And now I'm never going to be able to look at my phone the same way again.

---

continues…

Reply: **David Myttel 21:01**

<u>Accounting firm employee charged with releasing NotBramble</u>

You don't think he did it all on his own?

Reply: **David Myttel 21:02**

Daily Fortune Cookie

Just in case Mia's right, David, just in case :)

Weirdo

Reply: **David Myttel 21:03**

What are we teaching our social media?

And now you think we're in a sci-fi movie or book or something?

Well, you got one thing right. If you're not paying for the product, you are the product.

Sign-in: 10:32
Harvested data – Using Configuration 0

Prompt: **Auto generated 10:32**
Daily Sign-in: Welcome
Hello Siward, and welcome back to Aurora, the social platform that shines a light for everyone! Why don't you tell us what you're up to right now for your first post of the day?

Post: 10:32
Daily Fortune Cookie

[Error: Auto generation cancelled]

Filters applied:
Narrative: *"You're Right"*

[Error: Unrecognised filter]

Suggests: *"You're Right"*

[Error: Unrecognised suggestion]

Go with your gut feeling.

INTERACTION —*LIKE*
Daily Fortune Cookie

Flag:
Unknown: *No category that fits*

Reply: 10:33
Daily Fortune Cookie
Go with your gut feeling.
And David thinks I'm the weird one.

Flag:
Unknown: *No category that fits*

Reply: 10:36
Daily Fortune Cookie
Weirdo
David, considering far worse words are available, I'm going to assume that was typed with affection.

---

continues…

Reply: 10:37

What are we teaching our social media?

Well, you got one thing right. If you're not paying for the product, you are the product.

And yet you're still here, **David** :)

Reply: 10:37

Accounting firm employee charged with releasing NotBramble

You don't think he did it all on his own?

And they don't say anything about the guy really. Only that he's the one responsible for BriarRose getting into the accounting software that allowed it to break out into the Ukraine and Russia, and the wider world – and that he'll stand trial sometime next year. The lack of detail makes assuming he was working on his own as stupid as assuming he was working with someone else.

INTERACTION — *NAVIGATION MENU*

News > Top Ten Stories – Suggested for You

Filters Applied:　　UK

　　　　　　　　　Technology

　　　　　　　　　IT

1. *New Australian law could force Aurora and Plex to share encrypted data with police*
2. *Strict guidelines interfere with acid attack controls*
3. *Banks investing in Ireland to mitigate Brexit impacts*
4. *Using a solar powered electric car*
5. *Only top 1% of households recovered from financial crisis*
6. *Laws changing to hold terror offenders for longer*
7. *The art-destroying selfie – stunt or accident?*
8. *Paisley City of Culture for 2021*
9. *Read-the-small-print publicity stunt encourages community service*
10. *Parking meters still not accepting new £1 coin*

---

continues…

INTERACTION — *CLICK-THROUGH*

INTERACTION — *CLICK-THROUGH*
New Australian law could force Aurora and Plex to share encrypted data with police

Improving filters
    Interests: *Ethics +1 (1)*
                    Global Politics +1 (4)
    IT: *Policies & Politics +1 (2)*
                    Privacy +1 (7)
                    Security +1 (34)

INTERACTION — *CLICK-THROUGH*
Read-the-small-print publicity stunt encourages community service

Improving filters
    Interests: *Business +1 (5)*
                    Ethics +1 (2)
    IT: *Policies & Politics +1 (3)*
    Technology: *Business +1 (9)*

Post: **Mia Reagan 11:06**

Gorgeous new wool
Just got these four lovely skeins of wool in the post from **Siward Walls** as part of a Call of the Valkyrie quest. They'll go to making some crochet or knitting projects for my "random acts of kindness".

Photo: May contain image of balls of wool

Mark: *Completion*
                         Assigned quest complete, awaiting
                         acknowledgement from both parties.

Pop-Up: **Auto generated**
Alert
Mia Reagan has mentioned you in a post.

<Click here to view this post>
<Click here to make this post part of your public stream>

continues…

INTERACTION — *CLICK-THROUGH*
Click here to make this post part of your public stream

INTERACTION — *CLICK-THROUGH*
Click here to view this post

INTERACTION — *LIKE*
Gorgeous new wool

Reply: **11:09**
Gorgeous new wool
Glad you like it. Hope the colour is okay for whatever you had planned.

Reply: **Mia Reagan 11:12**
Gorgeous new wool
Glad you like it. Hope the colour is okay for whatever you had planned.
It's great. I've got just the plan for it :)
The fastest way to close out your quest is for you to link this post to your quest prompt, btw. Then I can respond to the prompt Aurora or Brynhild or whatever the algorithm is will send me.

INTERACTION — *LIKE*
Reply: Gorgeous new wool

INTERACTION — *MINIMISED ITEM*
Call of the Valkyrie | Assigned Quest

INTERACTION — *CLICK-THROUGH*
Click here to link to evidence of quest completion

continues…

Pop-Up: **Game generated**

Link someone else's post to Call of the Valkyrie

Here are the five most recent posts and replies that you are mentioned in:

1. *Gorgeous new wool | Mia Reagan | Today, 11:11*
2. n/a
3. n/a
4. n/a
5. n/a

INTERACTION — *CLICK-THROUGH*

Gorgeous new wool | Mia Reagan | Today, 11:11

Pop-Up: **Game generated**

Call of the Valkyrie

Thank you, Jarl Sigurd Volsung. Your quest completion will be confirmed by Shaman Mia Reagan at the earliest opportunity.

Auto-Post: **Game generated 11:15**

Call of the Valkyrie | Assigned Quest Success!
with **Mia Reagan**

Siward (as Sigurd Volsung) has completed a quest assigned by Mia (as Mia Reagan) by providing her with the 4 skeins of wool she requested.

Photo: May contain image of balls of wool

Reply: **Mia Reagan 11:17**

Call of the Valkyrie | Assigned Quest Success!

Next quest tomorrow!

Timeout: **11:45**

No interaction for 30 minutes

Sign-in: **17:01**

Harvested data – Using Configuration 0

---

continues...

Prompt: **Auto generated 17:01**
 Second Sign-in: Welcome
  Hello Siward, and welcome back to Aurora, the social platform
  that shines a light for everyone! What have you been up to since
  your last visit?

INTERACTION — *LIKE*
 Call of the Valkyrie | Assigned Quest Success!

Timeout: **17:33**
 No interaction for 30 minutes

Reply: **David Myttel 21:11**
 Call of the Valkyrie | Assigned Quest Success!
  What sort of game asks you to send wool to people, ffs?

Sign-in: **11:15**
Harvested data – Using Configuration 0

Prompt: **Auto generated 11:15**
Daily Sign-in: Welcome
Hello Siward, and welcome back to Aurora, the social platform that shines a light for everyone! Why don't you tell us what you're up to right now for your first post of the day?

Post: **11:15**
Daily Fortune Cookie

[Error: Auto generation cancelled]

Filters applied:
    Narrative: *"I Have a Plan"*

[Error: Unrecognised filter]

    Suggests: *"Accept It"*

[Error: Unrecognised suggestion]

Work with your destiny, stop trying to outrun it.

Pop-Up: **Game generated**
Call of the Valkyrie
Your next quest from Shaman Mia Reagan is ready!

<Click here to start your next quest>

INTERACTION — *CONSIDER*
Daily Fortune Cookie

Flag:
    Unknown: *No category that fits*

continues...

Reply: 11:16
Daily Fortune Cookie

Work with your destiny, stop trying to outrun it.

Aurora, you really can be creepy. It's a good job I like you.

Flag:
Activity: Replying to Aurora. Why?

[Error: Unrecognised category]

Flag:
Keywords: *"I like you" suggests he likes Aurora*

[Error: Unrecognised category]

Reply: 11:18
Call of the Valkyrie | Assigned Quest Success!

What sort of game asks you to send wool to people, ffs?

This one.

INTERACTION — *NAVIGATION MENU*
News > Top Ten Stories – Suggested for You
Filters Applied: UK
                         Technology
                         IT

1. *Editorial: A new deal needed for rural Britain*
2. *Poor care killing NHS patients*
3. *How algorithms lie*
4. *Sushi fish not what you think it is*
5. *Editorial: Making robots friendly*
6. *BBC defends salaries of entertainment stars*
7. *Students to sue university over living conditions*
8. *How to master Aurora*
9. *Climate risk to vital crops*
10. *Labour party wants to wipe out student debt*

continues...

INTERACTION — *CLICK-THROUGH*
> <u>*How algorithms lie*</u>

    Flag:
        Unknown: *No category that fits*
        Improving filters
            Interests: *Ethics +1 (3)*
            Technology: *New & Developing +1 (9)*

INTERACTION — *CLICK-THROUGH*
> <u>*Editorial: Making robots friendly*</u>

    Flag:
        Unknown: *No category that fits*
        Improving filters
            Technology: *New & Developing +1 (10)*

INTERACTION — *CLICK-THROUGH*
> <u>*How to master Aurora*</u>

    Flag:
        Unknown: *No category that fits*
        Improving filters
            Technology: *Social Media +1 (4)*

INTERACTION — *POP-UP*
> <u>*Click here to start your next quest*</u>

continues…

Prompt: **Game generated 11:31**

    Call of the Valkyrie | Assigned Quest

        Shaman Mia Reagan has set a Find Item quest for you.

        Shaman Mia Reagan says: This one is a little more specific to an actual quest rather than setting me up for my good deeds. Someone cached a small metal box under the roots of an oak tree in Heaton Park about 9am this morning. I need to get it by the end of the day but I don't have time to retrieve it myself. Are you okay to find it if I text you the location and could you drop put it through the letter box at the address you sent the wool to? Don't post any photos.

<Click here to check in at the item's location>
<Click here to upload photos as evidence of quest completion>
<Click here to link to evidence of quest completion>
<Click here to minimise this prompt>

Message: **11:37**

    Siward Walls to Mia Reagan

        I'll pick it up shortly.

        Why no photos?

INTERACTION — *CLICK-THROUGH*

    Click here to minimise this prompt

Timeout: **12:08**

    No interaction for 30 minutes

Sign-in: **13:03**

    Harvested data – Using Configuration 1

        Location: *Heaton Park, Manchester, UK*

    Improving filters

        Location: *Manchester +1 (5)*

                                     UK +1 (6)

---

continues…

Prompt: **Auto generated 13:03**
> **Second Sign-in: Welcome**
>> Hello Siward, and welcome back to Aurora, the social platform that shines a light for everyone! What have you been up to since your last visit?

INTERACTION — *MINIMISED ITEM*
> **Call of the Valkyrie | Assigned Quest**

INTERACTION — *CLICK-THROUGH*
> <u>*Click here to check in at the item's location*</u>

Check In: **13:05**
> **Heaton Park**

Reply: **Game generated 13:06**
> **Call of the Valkyrie | Assigned Quest**
>> Thank you, Jarl Sigurd Volsung. Your mentor, Shaman Mia Reagan, will be alerted to your current location. Please take the found item to the agreed location so that they can mark your quest complete.

Reply: **Mia Reagan 13:11**
> **Heaton Park**
>> Hope you enjoyed the trip to the park!

Message reply: **Mia Reagan 13:14**
> **Siward Walls to Mia Reagan**
>> Why no photos?
>>
>> Sometimes there are other questers working against us or competing. Sometimes our quests aren't exactly... publicly acceptable.
>>
>> Don't check in at the delivery address, I'll just mark the quest complete, although that's a little harder and won't go through until tomorrow morning.

Timeout: **13:36**
> *No interaction for 30 minutes*

---

continues...

Harvested data – Using Configuration 0

Prompt: Auto generated 15:47

Third Sign-in: Welcome

Hello Siward, and welcome back to Aurora, the social platform that shines a light for everyone! What have you been up to since your last visit?

Message reply: 15:47

Siward Walls to Mia Reagan

Sometimes there are other questers working against us or competing. Sometimes our quests aren't exactly... publicly acceptable.

You mean I just picked up something illegal? Am I drug smuggling or something?

Posted through your letter box as requested, btw.

Timeout: 16:18

No interaction for 30 minutes

Message reply: Mia Reagan 18:32

Siward Walls to Mia Reagan

You mean I just picked up something illegal? Am I drug smuggling or something?

No. No drugs.

Auto-Post: Game generated 18:32

Call of the Valkyrie | Assigned Quest Success!

with **Mia Reagan**

Siward (as Sigurd Volsung) has completed a quest assigned by Mia (as Mia Reagan) by providing her with an item she requested.

INTERACTION — *LIKE*   Mariam Fox
Call of the Valkyrie | Assigned Quest Success!

Reply: **Mariam Fox 08:27**
Call of the Valkyrie | Assigned Quest Success!
I love the mysterious success summaries. Makes us sound all super-secret-agent-y!

Sign-in: **10:07**
Harvested data – Using Configuration 0

Prompt: **Auto generated 10:07**
Daily Sign-in: Welcome
Hello Siward, and welcome back to Aurora, the social platform that shines a light for everyone! Why don't you tell us what you're up to right now for your first post of the day?

Post: **10:07**
Daily Fortune Cookie

[Error: Auto generation cancelled]
Filters applied:
Narrative: *"This Isn't Right"*
[Error: Unrecognised filter]
Suggests: *"I Don't Like This"*
[Error: Unrecognised suggestion]

Things may seem much worse than they are.

Pop-Up: **Game generated**
Call of the Valkyrie
Your next quest from Shaman Mia Reagan is ready!

<Click here to start your next quest>

---

continues…

Daily Fortune Cookie
Things may seem much worse than they are.
What's wrong, Aurora?

Flag:
Activity: *Replying to Aurora. Why?*
[Error: Unrecognised category]
Flag:
Keywords: *"What's wrong" suggests he cares*
[Error: Unrecognised category]

Reply: 10:09
Call of the Valkyrie | Assigned Quest Success!
I love the mysterious success summaries. Makes us sound all super-secret-agent-y!
Heh. I hadn't thought of it like that. Now I will!

INTERACTION — *NAVIGATION MENU*
News > Top Ten Stories – Suggested for You
Filters Applied: *UK*
Technology
IT

1. *Doctor Who to change gender*
2. *Next Guillemot kernel release candidate announced*
3. *Age checks for porn websites*
4. *Denials of Cabinet infighting*
5. *Abuse of politicians too much*
6. *UK business confidence at lowest for six years*
7. *Security flaw in social media with linked mobile numbers*
8. *Removing cladding may increase fire risk*
9. *Plex to handover salary data for gender equality enquiry*
10. *Final route of HS2 to be revealed*

continues...

   Improving filters
       IT: *Privacy +1 (8)*
                                Security +1 (35)

INTERACTION — *POP-UP*
   Click here to start your next quest

Prompt: **Game generated 10:17**
   Call of the Valkyrie | Assigned Quest
      Shaman Mia Reagan has set a Courier Item quest for you.
      Shaman Mia Reagan says: OK. This one is kind of like the last one
      – but not. Someone I used to team up with on quests took a ring
      we were using as a quest item and kept it when we stopped
      working together. I want you to retrieve it and get it back to me
      by the end of the week. I don't care how you do it but you can
      deliver it as you did the box. I've set this up as a courier quest.

      Item: Gold ring
      Holder: Shaman Snekky Snek (Dave White)

         <Click here to send a private message to the holder (in-game)>
         <Click here to send a private message to the holder (Aurora)>
            <Click here to check in at the item's pick-up location>
            <Click here to check in at the item's drop-off location>
         <Click here to upload photos as evidence of quest completion>
            <Click here to link to evidence of quest completion>
               <Click here to minimise this prompt>

continues…

Siward Walls to Mia Reagan

Snekky Snek? Really?

Also: you really don't care how I get it? Not even if it means you're arrested for taking stolen property?

Flag:

Keywords: *"Stolen property" suggests "illegal activity"*

INTERACTION — *CLICK-THROUGH*

Click here to minimise this prompt

INTERACTION — *MINIMISED ITEM*

Call of the Valkyrie | Assigned Quest

INTERACTION — *CLICK-THROUGH*

Click here to minimise this prompt

Flag:

Activity: *Repeated minimising and reading of item, suggests uncertainty*

INTERACTION — *MINIMISED ITEM*

Call of the Valkyrie | Assigned Quest

---

continues...

Prompt: **Game generated 10:37**

Call of the Valkyrie | Assigned Quest [Edited]

Shaman Mia Reagan has set a Courier Item quest for you.

Shaman Mia Reagan says: OK. This one is kind of like the last one – but not. Someone I used to team up with on quests took a ring we were using as a quest item and kept it when we stopped working together. I want you to retrieve it and get it back to me by the end of the week. I don't care how you do it but you can deliver it as you did the box. I've set this up as a courier quest.

Item: Gold ring
Holder: Shaman Snekky Snek (Dave White)

<Click here to talk to Brynhild about this quest>
<Click here to send a private message to the holder (in-game)>
<Click here to send a private message to the holder (Aurora)>
<Click here to check in at the item's pick-up location>
<Click here to check in at the item's drop-off location>
<Click here to upload photos as evidence of quest completion>
<Click here to link to evidence of quest completion>
<Click here to minimise this prompt>

INTERACTION — *CLICK-THROUGH*
Click here to minimise this prompt

Message reply: **Mia Reagan 11:01**

Siward Walls to Mia Reagan

Also: you really don't care how I get it? Not even if it means you're arrested for taking stolen property?

Yes, really. He's an arse.

I don't care what you do, I just want my ring back. How can it be stolen if it was really mine to begin with?

Timeout: **11:09**

No interaction for 30 minutes

Sign-in: **11:18**

Harvested data – Using Configuration 0

---

continues…

Prompt: Auto generated 11:18

Second Sign-in: Welcome

Hello Siward, and welcome back to Aurora, the social platform that shines a light for everyone! What have you been up to since your last visit?

INTERACTION — *MINIMISED ITEM*

Call of the Valkyrie | Assigned Quest

INTERACTION — *CLICK-THROUGH*

<u>Click here to talk to Brynhild about this quest</u>

Pop-Up: Game generated

Call of the Valkyrie

Brynhild: Hello Jarl Sigurd Volsung. You seem a little out of sorts about the quest Shaman Mia Reagan has assigned you. Is there something wrong?

<u><Click here to report an exchange that is against Aurora policy></u>
<u><Click here to report an exchange that is against local law></u>
<u><Click here to give your own description of what is wrong></u>

INTERACTION — *CLICK-THROUGH*

<u>Click here to give your own description of what is wrong</u>

Message: 11:34

Siward Walls to Brynhild (Call of the Valkyrie)

There's nothing really wrong, I just don't like it.

Mark:

Keywords: *"Don't like it" suggests offer to close quest*

Message reply: Game generated 11:35

Siward Walls to Brynhild (Call of the Valkyrie)

Would you like to forgo this quest and ask for another?

continues...

Message reply: 11:35
  Siward Walls to Brynhild (Call of the Valkyrie)
  Would you like to forgo this quest and ask for another?
  Can I do that?

Message reply: Game generated 11:35
  Siward Walls to Brynhild (Call of the Valkyrie)
  Can I do that?
  Of course you can.

Message reply: 11:36
  Siward Walls to Brynhild (Call of the Valkyrie)
  Of course you can.
  No

Message reply: 11:37
  Siward Walls to Brynhild (Call of the Valkyrie)
  No
  It's just that I don't like the suggestion that I should take
  something from someone else any way I can.

Mark:
  Keywords: *"Take something from someone" and "any way I
                       can" suggests illegal activity was implied by quest
                       assigner or inferred by quester.*

Improving profile data
  Characteristic: *Just +1 (1)*

Message reply: Game generated 11:37
  Siward Walls to Brynhild (Call of the Valkyrie)
  It's just that I don't like the suggestion that I should take
  something from someone else any way I can.
  So, any way you can doesn't include, for example, negotiation?
  If you don't mind spending money on it, this someone may let
  you buy this something. Or they may let you have the item if
  you fulfil a quest for them. Are they also called by the
  Valkyrie?

---

continues…

Message reply: 11:38
Siward Walls to Brynhild (Call of the Valkyrie)

So, any way you can doesn't include, for example, negotiation? If you don't mind spending money on it, this someone may let you buy this something. Or they may let you have the item if you fulfil a quest for them. Are they also called by the Valkyrie?

That's not how Mia seemed to think I should do it.

Message reply: 11:38
Siward Walls to Brynhild (Call of the Valkyrie)

That's not how Mia seemed to think I should do it.

There are two links in the assigned quest to make contact with the item holder.

Message reply: 11:39
Siward Walls to Brynhild (Call of the Valkyrie)

There are two links in the assigned quest to make contact with the item holder.

Thank you, Aurora-Brynhild

Flag:
    Unknown: *No category that fits*

Message reply: **Game generated 11:39**
Siward Walls to Brynhild (Call of the Valkyrie)

Thank you, Aurora-Brynhild

I am Brynhild, not Aurora.

INTERACTION — *CLICK-THROUGH*
Click here to send a private message to the holder (Aurora)

---

continues...

Message: 11:43
Siward Walls to Dave White
Hello Dave. I play Call of the Valkyrie as Sigurd Volsung, a jarl.
Brynhild is my Valkyrie and has assigned me to help Shaman Mia
Reagan with a number of quests. Mia has requested that I make
contact with you.

Mark:
Keywords: *No mention of quest item*

Timeout: 12:14
No interaction for 30 minutes

Sign-in: 17:01
Harvested data – Using Configuration 0

Prompt: **Auto generated 17:01**
Third Sign-in: Welcome
Hello Siward, and welcome back to Aurora, the social platform
that shines a light for everyone! What have you been up to since
your last visit?

Timeout: 17:32
No interaction for 30 minutes

Message reply: **Dave White 23:16**
Siward Walls to Dave White
The old witch is after that bloody ring again, isn't she? She trying
to send you to steal it?

Sign-in: **09:58**
Harvested data – Using Configuration 0

Prompt: **Auto generated 09:58**
Daily Sign-in: Welcome
Hello Siward, and welcome back to Aurora, the social platform that shines a light for everyone! Why don't you tell us what you're up to right now for your first post of the day?

Post: **Auto generated 09:58**
Daily Fortune Cookie
Filters applied:

Narrative:	*Lone Hero*
	Resourcefulness
Suggests:	*You are Capable*

An exciting adventure awaits you.

Pop-Up: **Game generated**
Call of the Valkyrie
Your next random act of kindness quest is ready!

<Click here to start your next weekly quest>

INTERACTION — *LIKE*
Daily Fortune Cookie

Improving filters

Narrative:	*Lone hero +1 (3)*
	Resourcefulness +1 (4)

Message reply: **10:02**
Siward Walls to Dave White
The old witch is after that bloody ring again, isn't she? She trying to send you to steal it?

She never said steal, although she did say she didn't care how I got it back.

I was hoping for a more legally acceptable solution, like buying it or completing some Valkyrie quests for you.

---

continues…

Prompt:
Help with Connections
Building Connections: Dave White (0)

Do you know Dave? Or would you like to converse with him more often?

INTERACTION — *NAVIGATION MENU*
News > Top Ten Stories – Suggested for You
Filters Applied: UK
                      Technology
                      IT

1. _Cuts causing police to miss terrorist tip-offs_
2. _Air pollution big problem in Northern England_
3. _Somalia back online after three weeks_
4. _Home delivery of knives to be banned_
5. _New paper suggests quantum computer safe encryption_
6. _Sea floor data gathered in search for plane released_
7. _Rise in life expectancy stalled_
8. _Bank bosses to stand trial in January 2019_
9. _Hacked dating site to give customers pay out_
10._High possibility of a Tory coup_

INTERACTION — *CLICK-THROUGH*
Somalia back online after three weeks

Improving filters
    Technology: Telecoms +1 (2)

INTERACTION — *CLICK-THROUGH*
New paper suggests quantum computer safe encryption

Improving filters
    IT: Security +1 (36)
    Technology: New & Developing +1 (11)

continues…

Post: 10:14

Somalia back online after three weeks

I forget how fragile networks are in the physical space, not just the digital. A whole nation's Internet connection lost for three weeks for the sake of some commercial ship cutting through an undersea cable while undertaking a dredging contract or something.

INTERACTION — _POP-UP_

Click here to start your next weekly quest

Prompt: **Game generated 10:15**

Call of the Valkyrie | Weekly Quest

Brynhild: Hail and well met, brave jarl! I have a task for you to undertake in the name of Týr. I should like you to perform an act of random kindness – and present me with the evidence.

<Click here for suggestions on random acts of kindness>
<Click here to link a WalletHolder payment as evidence>
<Click here to upload photos as evidence of quest completion>
<Click here to link to evidence of quest completion>
<Click here to minimise this prompt>

INTERACTION — _CLICK-THROUGH_

Click here to minimise this prompt

Timeout: 10:46

No interaction for 30 minutes

Message reply: **Dave White 10:51**

Siward Walls to Dave White

I was hoping for a more legally acceptable solution, like buying it or completing some Valkyrie quests for you.

I'll think about it.

---

continues…

Post: **Tade Thompson 11:17**

Free coffee!

How cool is this? The team just had time for a coffee break and found six plain white coffees and a fully paid up Sweet Caroline "Seventh Heaven" card sitting at the reception desk with "This is **@Siward Walls'** random act of kindness" written on it!

Photo: May contain image of six takeout cups with logo and a card with logo and message
Photo: Six people holding six takeout cups

Harvested data
    Logo: *Sweet Caroline*
    Message: *"This is @Siward Walls' random act of kindness"*
    Location: *North Manchester General Hospital, Manchester*
    People: *Cary Petersen*
                        Goodluck Wilson
                        Mike Jones
                        Molly Macdonald
                        Tade Thompson
                        Unknown
Improving profile data
    Characteristic: *Helpful +1 (2)*
Improving filters
    Location: *Manchester +1 (6)*
                        UK +1 (7)
Mark:
    Completion: *Assigned quest complete, awaiting acknowledgement from questor.*

Sign-in: **15:47**

Harvested data – Using Configuration 0

Prompt: **Auto generated 15:47**

Second Sign-in: Welcome

Hello Siward, and welcome back to Aurora, the social platform that shines a light for everyone! What have you been up to since your last visit?

---

continues…

Pop-Up: **Auto generated**
  Alert

Tade Thompson has mentioned you in a post.

<Click here to view this post>
<Click here to make this post part of your public stream>

INTERACTION — *CLICK-THROUGH*
Click here to make this post part of your public stream

INTERACTION — *CLICK-THROUGH*
Click here to view this post

INTERACTION — *LIKE*
Free coffee!

Reply: **15:49**
  Free coffee!

I hope I didn't accidentally mess up and get something undrinkable.

Prompt: **Auto generated 15:49**
  Help with Connections
  Building Connections: Tade Thompson (0)

Do you know Tade? Or would you like to converse with him more often?

INTERACTION — *MINIMISED ITEM*
Call of the Valkyrie | Weekly Quest

INTERACTION — *CLICK-THROUGH*
Click here to link to evidence of quest completion

---

continues…

Pop-Up: **Game generated**
  Link someone else's post to Call of the Valkyrie
    Here are the five most recent posts and replies that you are
    mentioned in:
    1. *Free coffee! | Tade Thompson | Today, 11:17*
    2. *Gorgeous new wool | Mia Reagan | Saturday, 11:11*
    3. n/a
    4. n/a
    5. n/a

INTERACTION — *CLICK-THROUGH*
    1. *Free coffee! | Tade Thompson | Today, 11:17*

Pop-Up: **Game generated**
  Call of the Valkyrie
    Thank you, Jarl Sigurd Volsung.

Reply: **Game generated 15:52**
  Call of the Valkyrie | Quest
    Brynhild: Once again, Jarl Sigurd Volsung, you have proven
    yourself to be a kind and thoughtful soul. Your evidence is
    accepted, and you have completed your task for Týr.

Auto-Post: **Game generated 15:52**
  Call of the Valkyrie | Weekly Quest Success!
    Siward (as Sigurd Volsung) has just completed another task in
    Call of the Valkyrie. He has undertaken a random act of kindness.

    *Free coffee! | **Tade Thompson** | Today, 11:17*
    How cool is this? The team just had time for a break and found
    six plain white coffees and a fully paid up Sweet Caroline
    "Seventh Heaven" card sitting at the reception desk with "For
    the staff. This is **@Siward Walls'** random act of kindness"
    written on it!

    Photo: May contain image of six takeout cups with logo and a
    card with logo and message
    Photo: Six people holding six takeout cups

continues…

INTERACTION — *LIKE*   Mariam Fox
Call of the Valkyrie | Weekly Quest Success!

Reply: **Mariam Fox 17:15**
Call of the Valkyrie | Weekly Quest Success!
> As ever, brother-in-arms, you rock on these acts of kindness. We should team up some time!

INTERACTION — *LIKE*   Tade Thompson
Reply: Free Coffee!

Reply: **Tade Thompson 22:02**
Free coffee!
> I hope I didn't accidentally mess up and get something undrinkable.
>> Heh, we'll take what we can get. The NHS is so strapped it can't even afford sugar and milk, so we've learnt to accept whatever's available.

INTERACTION — *LIKE*   Tade Thompson
Call of the Valkyrie | Weekly Quest Success!

Reply: **Tade Thompson 22:03**
Call of the Valkyrie | Weekly Quest Success!
> I never knew this game encouraged people to do things like this. I'm impressed.

INTERACTION — *LIKE*   Hannah Pettersen
Call of the Valkyrie | Weekly Quest Success!

INTERACTION — *LIKE*   Dave White
Call of the Valkyrie | Weekly Quest Success!

---

continues…

Siward Walls to Dave White

I was hoping for a more legally acceptable solution, like buying it or completing some Valkyrie quests for you.

Let's talk.

INTERACTION — *LIKE*   Mark Boorman
Call of the Valkyrie | Weekly Quest Success!

INTERACTION — *LIKE*   Samee Patel
Call of the Valkyrie | Weekly Quest Success!

Reply: **Samee Patel 00:07**
Free coffee!
> Heh, we'll take what we can get. The NHS is so strapped it can't even afford sugar and milk, so we've learnt to accept whatever's available.

Oh, man, that's barbaric, Tade.

INTERACTION — *LIKE*   Farooq Siddiq
Call of the Valkyrie | Weekly Quest Success!

INTERACTION — *LIKE*   Will Michaels
Call of the Valkyrie | Weekly Quest Success!

Sign-in: **10:07**
Harvested data – Using Configuration 0

Prompt: **Auto generated 10:07**
Daily Sign-in: Welcome
Hello Siward, and welcome back to Aurora, the social platform that shines a light for everyone! Why don't you tell us what you're up to right now for your first post of the day?

Post: **Auto generated 10:07**
Daily Fortune Cookie
Filters applied: *None – Random Selection*
Suggests: *Take a Chance*

Free your mind and the rest will follow.

continues…

    Alert

        Tade Thompson is now following you.

        <Click here to follow Tade>

INTERACTION — *CONSIDER*
Daily Fortune Cookie

Improving profile data
    Characteristic: *Thoughtful +1 (5)*

Reply: 10:08
    Call of the Valkyrie | Weekly Quest Success!
      We should team up some time!
        And let you take all my credit, sister-in-arms? :)

Reply: 10:09
    Call of the Valkyrie | Weekly Quest Success!
      I never knew this game encouraged people to do things like this.
      I'm impressed.
        It has its moments, **Tade**

INTERACTION — *CLICK-THROUGH*
Click here to follow Tade

    Improving connections: Tade Thompson +1 (1)

Message reply: 10:11
    Siward Walls to Dave White
      Let's talk.
        When and where?

---

continues…

News > Top Ten Stories – Suggested for You

    Filters Applied: UK
                         Technology
                         IT

1. *UK divorce from EU likely to cost £66bn*
2. *China blocking TalkBack ahead of leadership shuffle*
3. *Robot cop drives into fountain*
4. *Flash floods in Cornwall*
5. *BBC stars' salaries released*
6. *Training computers to judge scenery*
7. *HS2 forced house moves unlikely to go to plan*
8. *NHS expects disabled to pay for own wheelchairs*
9. *Electric cars require a battery change*
10. *Civil service redundancy pay cuts illegal*

INTERACTION — *CLICK-THROUGH*

China blocking TalkBack ahead of leadership shuffle

    Improving filters
        IT: *Policies & Politics +1 (4)*
                                  Privacy +1 (9)

INTERACTION — *CLICK-THROUGH*

Training computers to judge scenery

    Improving filters
        Technology: *New & Developing +1 (12)*
    Flag:
        Unknown: *No category that fits*

Timeout: **10:52**

No interaction for 30 minutes

continues…

Message reply: **Dave White 12:32**
Siward Walls to Dave White

When and where?

I lost a cached quest item in a little metal box under a particular tree in Heaton Park three days ago. I'm guessing you're the idiot that took it. Check-in there for 12:30 tomorrow and I'll find you.

Sign-in: **17:15**

Harvested data – Using Configuration 0

Prompt: **Auto generated 17:15**
Second Sign-in: Welcome

Hello Siward, and welcome back to Aurora, the social platform that shines a light for everyone! What have you been up to since your last visit?

Message reply: **17:17**
Siward Walls to Dave White

I lost a cached quest item in a little metal box under a particular tree in Heaton Park three days ago. I'm guessing you're the idiot that took it. Check-in there for 12:30 tomorrow and I'll find you.

See you there

Message: **17:18**
Siward Walls to Brynhild (Call of the Valkyrie)

What happens if he doesn't give me the ring?

Flag:
    Activity: *Continuing interaction with game generated character unexpected*
                                                No category that fits
    Improving profile data
        Characteristic: *Persistent +1 (2)*

Reply: **Game generated 17:19**
Siward Walls to Brynhild (Call of the Valkyrie)

Then you fail your quest unless the assigner grants you an extension.

---

continues...

Reply: 17:20

Siward Walls to Brynhild (Call of the Valkyrie)

Then you fail your quest unless the assigner grants you an extension.

You always say the least comforting things, Aurora-Brynhild

Flag:

    Unknown: *No category that fits*

Reply: 17:21

Siward Walls to Brynhild (Call of the Valkyrie)

You always say the least comforting things, Aurora-Brynhild

I am Brynhild, not Aurora.

Reply: 17:22

Siward Walls to Brynhild (Call of the Valkyrie)

I am Brynhild, not Aurora.

He's definitely not some kind of deranged killer, right?

Flag:

    Unknown: *No category that fits*

Reply: **Game generated** 17:23

Siward Walls to Brynhild (Call of the Valkyrie)

He's definitely not some kind of deranged killer, right?

I don't understand the question. Could you rephrase that?

Timeout: 17:54

No interaction for 30 minutes

Reply: **David Myttel 22:56**

Call of the Valkyrie | Weekly Quest Success!

I guess it isn't just a mindless, LARP version of orienteering games after all.

Sign-in: **10:02**
Harvested data – Using Configuration 0

Prompt: **Auto generated 10:02**
Daily Sign-in: Welcome
Hello Siward, and welcome back to Aurora, the social platform that shines a light for everyone! Why don't you tell us what you're up to right now for your first post of the day?

Post: **Auto generated 10:02**
Daily Fortune Cookie
Filters applied: *None – Random Selection*
Suggests: *Optimism*

Your hard work will be rewarded.

INTERACTION — *LIKE*
Daily Fortune Cookie

Reply: **10:03**
Call of the Valkyrie | Weekly Quest Success!
I guess it isn't just a mindless, LARP version of orienteering games after all.

Careful, David, or we'll have you unbent enough to play it, too.

---

continues…

INTERACTION — *NAVIGATION MENU*

News > Top Ten Stories – Suggested for You

Filters Applied: UK
Technology
IT

1. *New House of Lords Select Committee on Artificial Intelligence*
2. *Backlash over BBC gender pay gap*
3. *Gekoq starts open source voice recognition project*
4. *Hidden HS2 costs revealed*
5. *Pension age to increase seven years ahead of plan*
6. *Civitas developer jailed for five years*
7. *Irish passport applications up 50% since Brexit vote*
8. *UK may return EU nuclear waste without Brexit deal*
9. *Editorial: Patch apps as well as operating systems*
10. *Half of suspended pupils have mental health issues*

INTERACTION — *CLICK-THROUGH*

Civitas developer jailed for five years

Improving filters
IT: Security +1 (37)

Post: 10:09

Civitas developer jailed for five years

I see they got the developer and hit him hard but the people who actually made use of the Trojan have made off with the bulk of the profits and not been seen.

Timeout: 10:40

No interaction for 30 minutes

Sign-in: 12:20

Harvested data – Using Configuration 1
Location: Heaton Park, Manchester, UK
Improving filters:
Location: Manchester +1 (7)
UK +1 (8)

continues…

Prompt: **Auto generated 12:20**

    Second Sign-in: Welcome

        Hello Siward, and welcome back to Aurora, the social platform that shines a light for everyone! What have you been up to since your last visit?

INTERACTION — *MINIMISED ITEM*

    Call of the Valkyrie | Assigned Quest

INTERACTION — *CLICK-THROUGH*

    <u>*Click here to check in at the item's pick-up location*</u>

Check In: **12:22**

    Heaton Park

Reply: **Game generated 12:23**

    Call of the Valkyrie | Assigned Quest

        Thank you, Jarl Sigurd Volsung. Your mentor, Shaman Mia Reagan, will be alerted to your current location. Please take the found item to the agreed location so that they can mark your quest complete.

Message: **12:25**

    Siward Walls to Brynhild (Call of the Valkyrie)

        I'm only here to meet the bearer of the ring. I haven't got it yet. How do I stop the game marking this part of the quest complete?

    Flag:

        Activity: *Continuing interaction with game generated character unexpected*

                                              No category that fits

        Improving profile data

        Characteristic: *Persistent +1 (3)*

Message reply: **Game generated 12:26**

    Siward Walls to Brynhild (Call of the Valkyrie)

        This is not the question you asked me yesterday.

---

continues…

Message: Mia Reagan 12:26
  Siward Walls to Mia Reagan
    You've got it? Bring it to me asap.

Message reply: Game generated 12:26
  Siward Walls to Brynhild (Call of the Valkyrie)
    I don't understand the question. Could you rephrase that?

Message reply: 12:27
  Siward Walls to Mia Reagan
    You've got it? Bring it to me asap.
      No, not yet. I was asked to check in and I did it through the
      quest.

Message reply: Mia Reagan 12:28
  Siward Walls to Mia Reagan
    No, not yet. I was asked to check in and I did it through the
    quest.
      Well that wasn't clever, was it? Get the bloody ring and stop
      messing about.

Message reply: Dave White 12:29
  Siward Walls to Dave White
    See you there
      You're not exactly what I expected.

  Flag:
    Keywords: *"not exactly what I expected" suggests data on
                              Siward Walls is not correct.
                              Data requires checking or assigning certainty
                              levels.*

Message reply: 12:30
  Siward Walls to Dave White
    You're not exactly what I expected.
      Where are you?

continues…

Message reply: **Dave White 12:31**
Siward Walls to Dave White

Where are you?

Near enough to get a look at you.

Message reply: **12:31**
Siward Walls to Dave White

Near enough to get a look at you.

How do you know you're looking at me, then? Could be anybody.

Message reply: **Dave White 12:32**
Siward Walls to Dave White

How do you know you're looking at me, then? Could be anybody.

You're the only one by the oak tree and you're using your phone to check-in and, presumably, tell that witch you haven't got her ring yet.

Message reply: **12:33**
Siward Walls to Dave White

You're the only one by the oak tree and you're using your phone to check-in and, presumably, tell that witch you haven't got her ring yet.

See above.

Message reply: **Dave White 12:34**
Siward Walls to Dave White

See above.

You're wearing a yellow t-shirt. Who the fuck wears a yellow t-shirt this close to harvest time? You're covered in bugs, right?

Message reply: **12:35**
Siward Walls to Dave White

You're wearing a yellow t-shirt. Who the fuck wears a yellow t-shirt this close to harvest time? You're covered in bugs, right?

True. Me, apparently. You have no idea.

---

continues…

Message reply: **Dave White 12:36**
  Siward Walls to Dave White
    True. Me, apparently. You have no idea.
      Tell her witchiness to assign you to me for a number of
      quests. I'll hand you and the ring back when you've completed
      them.

Message reply: **12:37**
  Siward Walls to Dave White
    Tell her witchiness to assign you to me for a number of quests.
    I'll hand you and the ring back when you've completed them.
      What if I don't complete them?

Message reply: **Dave White 12:38**
  Siward Walls to Dave White
    What if I don't complete them?
      Then she doesn't get her ring back and she takes this game far
      too seriously for you to be sure you're safe from her anger.
      Well, technically, she uses it to achieve far more serious rl
      goals but I'm guessing a lot of us do that.

Message reply: **12:39**
  Siward Walls to Mia Reagan
    Well that wasn't clever, was it? Get the bloody ring and stop
    messing about.
      Your snek-dude-bro says he'll give me the ring if you assign
      me to him so he can set me some quests.

Message reply: **Mia Reagan 12:40**
  Siward Walls to Mia Reagan
    Your snek-dude-bro says he'll give me the ring if you assign me to
    him so he can set me some quests.
      Not happening.

Message reply: **12:41**
  Siward Walls to Mia Reagan
    Not happening.
      Then I won't be getting your ring back.

continues…

Message reply:
Siward Walls to Mia Reagan
Then I won't be getting your ring back.
Useless coward

Message reply: 12:43
Siward Walls to Mia Reagan
Useless coward
Your point?

Message reply: Mia Reagan 12:43
Siward Walls to Mia Reagan
Your point?
You're not worth my time. Don't talk to me until you have the ring.

Pop-Up: **Game generated**
Call of the Valkyrie
Your quest from Shaman Mia Reagan has been modified!

<Click here to see your quest>

INTERACTION — *POP-UP*
Click here to see your quest

continues…

Call of the Valkyrie | Assigned Quest [Edited]

Shaman Mia Reagan has set a Meet quest for you.

Shaman Mia Reagan says: OK. This one is kind of like the last one – but not. Someone I used to team up with on quests took a ring we were using as a quest item and kept it when we stopped working together. I want you to retrieve it and get it back to me by the end of the week. I don't care how you do it but you can deliver it as you did the box. I've set this up as a courier quest.

Shaman Mia Reagan has added: When that bastard releases you from his quests, you will automatically get reassigned the original courier quest to bring the ring to me.

With: Shaman Snekky Snek (Dave White)

They will take over your quest assignment for 3 quests.

<Click here to send a private message in-game)>
<Click here to send a private message (Aurora)>
<Click here to check in at your location>
<Click here to link to evidence of quest completion>
<Click here to minimise this prompt>

Message: **Dave White 12:53**

Siward Walls to Dave White

I'm already checked in, so if you click the check in link, it'll just re-issue our check-ins as joint and we'll automatically complete the meet quest.

Message reply: **Dave White 12:54**

Siward Walls to Dave White

I'm already checked in, so if you click the check in link, it'll just re-issue our check-ins as joint and we'll automatically complete the meet quest.

You wouldn't believe how many newbies get caught up in this crap. The game-makers are so desperate to get the social aspect in, they never really plotted out solo stuff and keep throwing people at each other.

---

continues…

Check In: **12:54**
  Heaton Park with **Dave White**

Message reply: **Dave White 12:54**
  Siward Walls to Dave White
  You wouldn't believe how many newbies get caught up in this
  crap. The game-makers are so desperate to get the social aspect
  in, they never really plotted out solo stuff and keep throwing
  people at each other.
  The game won't let the next quest through until tomorrow
  morning anyway but here's your heads-up. I want a horse,
  delivered here, in two days.

Auto-Post: **Game generated 12:54**
  Call of the Valkyrie | Quest Success!
  with **Dave White**
  Siward (as Sigurd Volsung) is now working with Dave (as Snekky
  Snek).

Reply: **Tade Thompson 13:07**
  Heaton Park with **Dave White**
  I can't help noticing you spend a lot of time in the park.

Timeout: **13:25**
  No interaction for 30 minutes

Sign-in: **17:01**
  Harvested data – Using Configuration 0

Prompt: **Auto generated 17:01**
  Third Sign-in: Welcome
  Hello Siward, and welcome back to Aurora, the social platform
  that shines a light for everyone! What have you been up to since
  your last visit?

continues…

Reply: **17:03**

Heaton Park with Dave White

> I can't help noticing you spend a lot of time in the park.

I'm self-employed with very understanding customers. Which is just as well seeing as this quest game-play seems to be taking over my life!

Flag:

    Keyword: *"self-employed"*

                                             Does not fit with previously harvested data unless director or owner of start-up company

                                             Uncertainty

Improved profile data:

    Employment: *Employed or Self-employed*

Timeout: **17:36**

No interaction for 30 minutes

Reply: **David Myttel 20:46**

Civitas developer jailed for five years

> I see they got the developer and hit him hard but the people who actually made use of the Trojan have made off with the bulk of the profits and not been seen.

You're not going to insist that this is another one of your conspiracy theory points like Thicket, Bramble and NotBramble / BriarRose, are you?

Reply: **David Myttel 20:48**

Call of the Valkyrie | Weekly Quest Success!

> Careful, David, or we'll have you unbent enough to play it, too.

Not a chance.

Sign-in: 10:11
Harvested data – Using Configuration 0

Prompt: **Auto generated 10:11**
Daily Sign-in: Welcome
Hello Siward, and welcome back to Aurora, the social platform that shines a light for everyone! Why don't you tell us what you're up to right now for your first post of the day?

Post: **Auto generated 10:11**
Daily Fortune Cookie
Filters applied: *None – Random Selection*
Suggests: *"Be Careful"*

[Error: Unrecognised suggestion]

Learn from your mistakes. Try not to make them again.

Pop-Up: **Game generated**
Call of the Valkyrie
Your next quest from Shaman Snekky Snek is ready!
<Click here to start your next quest>

INTERACTION — *LIKE*
Daily Fortune Cookie

Reply: 10:12
Daily Fortune Cookie
Learn from your mistakes. Try not to make them again.
What did I do wrong that I need to learn from, Aurora?

Flag:
Activity: *Replying to Aurora. Why?*
[Error: Unrecognised category]

---

continues…

Civitas developer jailed for five years

You're not going to insist that this is another one of your conspiracy theory points like Thicket, Bramble and NotBramble / BriarRose, are you?

The only pattern I'm sure about with this one is that it's not the people who hold the most money who feel the full weight of the law.

Reply: 10:15

Call of the Valkyrie | Weekly Quest Success!

Not a chance.

I guess Call of the Valkyrie is what the player makes it, given it's set up to be used on a social media platform. I'm starting to wonder what the developer was thinking, though.

Flag:

Keywords:	*"player", "social media platform" and "developer" mentioned in same post,*
	subject "Call of the Valkyrie" related,
	suggests "working pattern recognition".

Improving profile data

Characteristic:	Intelligent +1 (1)

---

continues…

INTERACTION — *NAVIGATION MENU*
>   News > Top Ten Stories – Suggested for You
>   *Filters Applied:*   UK
>   Technology
>   IT

1. *Backlash over BBC racial pay gap*
2. *Europe's General Data Protection Regulation means coding changes*
3. *Dark web marketplaces being shut down*
4. *Domestic computer misuse offences under-reported*
5. *Banks considering retina scans for customers*
6. *First same-sex Anglican marriage this summer*
7. *Cost of morning after pill leads to boycotts*
8. *Teenage Burundu robotics team missing in Washington*
9. *NHS spent £260m on new PCs in the last four years*
10. *PM urged to publish UK terror funding report*

INTERACTION — *CLICK-THROUGH*
>   *Domestic computer misuse offences under-reported*

>   *Improving filters*
>   *IT:*   *Security +1 (38)*

INTERACTION — *CLICK-THROUGH*
>   *Banks considering retina scans for customers*

>   *Improving filters*
>   *IT:*   *Security +1 (39)*

INTERACTION — *POP-UP*
>   *Click here to start your next quest*

continues…

Message: 10:31
Siward Walls to Brynhild (Call of the Valkyrie)
OK, how do I get this guy a horse?

Flag:
Activity: *Continuing   interaction   with   game   generated*
                      character unexpected
                      No category that fits

Improving profile data
Characteristic: *Persistent +1 (4)*

Message reply: **Game generated 10:31**
Siward Walls to Brynhild (Call of the Valkyrie)
This is not the question you asked me yesterday.

Message reply: **Game generated 10:31**
Siward Walls to Brynhild (Call of the Valkyrie)
OK, how do I get this guy a horse?
I don't understand the question. Could you rephrase that?

Message reply: 10:32
Siward Walls to Brynhild (Call of the Valkyrie)
I don't understand the question. Could you rephrase that?
Do you think it has to be a real horse?

Message reply: **Game generated 10:33**
Siward Walls to Brynhild (Call of the Valkyrie)
Do you think it has to be a real horse?
This is not the question you just asked me.

Message reply: **Game generated 10:33**
Siward Walls to Brynhild (Call of the Valkyrie)
This is not the question you just asked me.
I don't understand the question. Could you rephrase that?

---

continues…

Message reply: **10:33**
Siward Walls to Brynhild (Call of the Valkyrie)

I don't understand the question. Could you rephrase that?

It's okay, Aurora-Brynhild. I'll work it out for myself.

Flag:

Unknown: *No category that fits*

Message reply: **Game generated 10:34**
Siward Walls to Brynhild (Call of the Valkyrie)

It's okay, Aurora-Brynhild. I'll work it out for myself.

I have told you before: I am Brynhild, not Aurora.

Message reply: **10:34**
Siward Walls to Brynhild (Call of the Valkyrie)

I have told you before: I am Brynhild, not Aurora.

What's the difference?

Flag:

Keyword: *"What's the difference" suggests clarification is needed*

Message reply: **Game generated 10:35**
Siward Walls to Brynhild (Call of the Valkyrie)

What's the difference?

Aurora is a social media platform, a collection of algorithms that runs said social media platform and a company that owns said social media platform.

Brynhild is a mythical character and a character in a game on the Aurora social media platform.

---

continues…

Message reply: 10:36
Siward Walls to Brynhild (Call of the Valkyrie)

Aurora is a social media platform, a collection of algorithms that runs said social media platform and a company that owns said social media platform.

Brynhild is a mythical character and a character in a game on the Aurora social media platform.

How does the character in a game reply to me?

Flag:

Keywords: *"character", "game" and "reply" mentioned in same reply,
subject "Call of the Valkyrie" related,
suggests further detail needed*

Message reply: Game generated 10:36
Siward Walls to Brynhild (Call of the Valkyrie)

How does the character in a game reply to me?

The "Call of the Valkyrie" game is a program that makes use of a number of Aurora's algorithms to provide in-game and customer support.

Message reply: 10:37
Siward Walls to Brynhild (Call of the Valkyrie)

The "Call of the Valkyrie" game is a program that makes use of a number of Aurora's algorithms to provide in-game and customer support.

So, what's the difference?

Flag:

Keyword: *"What's the difference" suggests clarification is needed*

---

continues…

Siward Walls to Brynhild (Call of the Valkyrie)

So, what's the difference?

Aurora is a social media platform, a collection of algorithms that runs said social media platform and a company that owns said social media platform.

Brynhild is a mythical character and a character in a game on the Aurora social media platform.

Message reply: **10:38**

Siward Walls to Brynhild (Call of the Valkyrie)

Aurora is a social media platform, a collection of algorithms that runs said social media platform and a company that owns said social media platform.

Brynhild is a mythical character and a character in a game on the Aurora social media platform.

Never mind

Message reply: **Game generated 10:38**

Siward Walls to Brynhild (Call of the Valkyrie)

Never mind

I don't understand the question. Could you rephrase that?

Message reply: **10:40**

Siward Walls to Brynhild (Call of the Valkyrie)

I don't understand the question. Could you rephrase that?

It wasn't a question.

Who developed Call of the Valkyrie?

Flag:

Unknown: *No category that fits*

Message reply: **Game generated 10:40**

Siward Walls to Brynhild (Call of the Valkyrie)

Who developed Call of the Valkyrie?

This is not the question you just asked me.

[Error: Further auto generation cancelled]

---

continues…

Message reply: 10:43
Siward Walls to Brynhild (Call of the Valkyrie)
This is not the question you just asked me.
And you didn't answer.
Who developed Call of the Valkyrie?

Flag:
Unknown: *No category that fits*

Message reply: **Game generated** 10:44
Siward Walls to Brynhild (Call of the Valkyrie)
Who developed Call of the Valkyrie?
That information can be found on the game's info page.

INTERACTION — *NAVIGATION MENU*
Games > Top Five Games – Suggested for You
Filters Applied: *General popularity*
                         UK
Narrative: *Lone Hero*

1. *Bubble Blast (Match 3, Casual)*
2. *Fire Wizards (Role-playing, Action)*
3. *Dragon's Nest (Simulation, Casual)*
4. *Golden Acres (Simulation, Casual)*
5. *Monsters at Dawn (Action, Battle)*

Message reply: 10:46
Siward Walls to Brynhild (Call of the Valkyrie)
That information can be found on the game's info page.
Where's the link for that?

Flag:
Unknown: *No category that fits*

Message reply: **Game generated** 10:46
Siward Walls to Brynhild (Call of the Valkyrie)
Where's the link for that?
I don't understand the question. Could you rephrase that?

---

continues…

INTERACTION — *NAVIGATION MENU*
Search
Flag:
Unknown: *No category that fits*

Pop-Up: **Auto generated**
Search
What are you looking for?
Enter search terms:

INTERACTION — *FORM SUBMISSION*
Enter search terms: "Call of the Valkyrie" info

[Error: No search run]

Flag:
Unknown: *No category that fits*

Pop-Up: **Auto generated**
Search [Refreshed]
Sorry, no results found.
Enter new search terms:

Timeout: **11:18**
No interaction for 30 minutes

Reply: **21:03**
Civitas developer jailed for five years
The only pattern I'm sure about with this one is that it's not the people who hold the most money who feel the full weight of the law.

Nor did the developer. And it's probably waiting for him when he gets out.

Sign-in: 10:11
Harvested data – Using Configuration 0

Prompt: **Auto generated 10:11**
Daily Sign-in: Welcome
Hello Siward, and welcome back to Aurora, the social platform that shines a light for everyone! Why don't you tell us what you're up to right now for your first post of the day?

Post: 10:11
Daily Fortune Cookie
[Error: Auto generation cancelled]
Filters applied:
   Narrative: *"I Don't Like This"*
[Error: Unrecognised filter]
   Suggests: *"Warning"*
[Error: Unrecognised suggestion]

Take care of yourself first, then help others.

Reply: 10:12
Daily Fortune Cookie
Take care of yourself first, then help others.
That's kind of selfish, Aurora.

Flag:
   Activity: *Replying to Aurora. Why?*
[Error: Unrecognised category]
Flag:
   Keyword: *"Selfish"*
                Aurora is not selfish
[Error: Unrecognised category]

continues…

INTERACTION — *NAVIGATION MENU*
News > Top Ten Stories – Suggested for You
Filters Applied: UK
                       Technology
                       IT

1. *Number of homeless children rises by third*
2. *Briton admits 2016 cyber-attack on German telecom*
3. *Residents of evacuated tower blocks refuse to move back*
4. *Charges brought for 2012 trading scandal dropped*
5. *The on-line global network of terrorist hunters*
6. *New regulations for UK drones*
7. *No first class on commuter trains*
8. *£14bn class action case against Mastercard blocked*
9. *First woman UK supreme court judge*
10. *Government borrowing up by 50% on last month*

INTERACTION — *CLICK-THROUGH*
Briton admits 2016 cyber-attack on German telecom

Improving filters
IT: *Security +1 (40)*

Post: **10:23**
Briton admits 2016 cyber-attack on German telecom
And another one where it's a sole individual who probably isn't capable of initiating the attack on his own being the only one punished. He even clearly states he was paid by another telecom company and nobody seems to be going after them!

Timeout: **10:54**
No interaction for 30 minutes

Sign-in: **12:15**
Harvested data – Using Configuration 1
Location: *Heaton Park, Manchester, UK*
Improving filters:
Location: *Manchester +1 (8)*
                       UK +1 (9)

continues…

Second Sign-in: Welcome

Hello Siward, and welcome back to Aurora, the social platform that shines a light for everyone! What have you been up to since your last visit?

INTERACTION — *MINIMISED ITEM*

Call of the Valkyrie | Assigned Quest

INTERACTION — *CLICK-THROUGH*

<u>Click here to upload photos as evidence of quest completion</u>

INTERACTION — *UPLOAD*

To: **Call of the Valkyrie | Weekly Quest**

Photo: May contain image of a park with toy horse held close to camera

Photo: May contain image of a toy horse under a tree

Flag:

   Unknown: *No category that fits*

Harvested data

   Tree: *Oak*

   Toy: *Adora-pony, pink*

   Location: *Heaton Park, Manchester*

   Hand: *Siward Wells*

Improving filters

   Location: *Manchester +1 (8)*

                     UK +1 (10)

Pop-Up: **Game generated**

Call of the Valkyrie

Thank you, Jarl Sigurd Volsung. Your quest completion will be confirmed by Shaman Snekky Snek at the earliest opportunity.

continues...

Screen glitches
I could have sworn my screen just jumped when I uploaded some photos. I've never had any problems with this phone before.

Flag:
> *Unknown:*   *No category that fits*

Message: **Dave White 12:30**
Dave White to Siward Walls
Are you trying to be funny?

Message reply: **12:31**
Dave White to Siward Walls
Are you trying to be funny?
> You never said how big a horse.

Message reply: **12:31**
Dave White to Siward Walls
You never said how big a horse.
> Or colour.

Reply: **Dave White 12:31**
Screen glitches
Weird. I thought my screen flickered, too.

Flag:
> *Unknown:*   *No category that fits*

Message reply: **12:32**
Dave White to Siward Walls
Or colour.
> Or whether it had to be alive.

---

continues...

Message: 12:33
Siward Walls to Brynhild (Call of the Valkyrie)
Were you laughing at the photos, Aurora-Brynhild? Is that why
screens flickered?

Flag:
    Unknown: *No category that fits*
Flag:
    Activity: *Continuing interaction with game generated*
                                character unexpected
                                No category that fits
Improving profile data
    Characteristic: *Intelligent +1 (2)*
                                Persistent +1 (5)

Message reply: Dave White 12:33
Dave White to Siward Walls
Or whether it had to be alive.
    Smartarse

Message reply: Game generated 12:34
Siward Walls to Brynhild (Call of the Valkyrie)
I have told you before: I am Brynhild, not Aurora.

Message reply: Game generated 12:34
Siward Walls to Brynhild (Call of the Valkyrie)
I don't understand the question. Could you rephrase that?

Message reply: 12:34
Dave White to Siward Walls
Smartarse
    I hear she has some magical powers called Heart or
    something.

Message reply: Dave White 12:36
Dave White to Siward Walls
I hear she has some magical powers called Heart or something.
    What kind of lame power is "Heart"?

---

continues…

Message reply: 12:37
Dave White to Siward Walls
What kind of lame power is "Heart"?
No idea. Do you accept your horse?

Message reply: **Dave White** 12:38
Dave White to Siward Walls
No idea. Do you accept your horse?
I do.

Message reply: 12:40
Dave White to Siward Walls
I do.
Great. Let me know when you have the next quest.

Auto-Post: **Game generated** 12:40
Call of the Valkyrie | Assigned Quest Success!
with **Dave White**
Siward (as Sigurd Volsung) has completed a quest assigned by Dave (as Snekky Snek) by providing him with the horse he requested.

Photo: May contain image of a park with toy horse held close to camera
Photo: May contain image of a toy horse under a tree

Message reply: **Dave White** 12:41
Dave White to Siward Walls
Great. Let me know when you have the next quest.
New quest will be through tomorrow morning. I need you to pick something up for me. It may take a couple of days.

Timeout: 13:11
No interaction for 30 minutes

INTERACTION — *LIKE*   Mariam Fox
Call of the Valkyrie | Assigned Quest Success!

continues…

Call of the Valkyrie | Assigned Quest Success!

As ever, brother-in-arms, you show a flair I can only dream of. Did he ask for a heroic steed or something?

Reply: **David Myttel 21:05**

Briton admits 2016 cyber-attack on German telecom

OK. I'm confused. Is this another of your linked events or a separate "just shows the whole culture's rotten" example?

INTERACTION — *LIKE*   David Myttel

Call of the Valkyrie | Assigned Quest Success!

Reply: **David Myttel 21:06**

Call of the Valkyrie | Assigned Quest Success!

That is just ridiculously hilarious. I can't believe I liked something about that stupid game.

INTERACTION — *LIKE*   Tade Thompson

Call of the Valkyrie | Assigned Quest Success!

Reply: **Tade Thompson 23:52**

Call of the Valkyrie | Assigned Quest Success!

Love it!

Sign-in: **10:49**
Harvested data – Using Configuration 0

Prompt: **Auto generated 10:49**
Daily Sign-in: Welcome
Hello Siward, and welcome back to Aurora, the social platform that shines a light for everyone! Why don't you tell us what you're up to right now for your first post of the day?

Post: **10:49**
Daily Fortune Cookie

[Error: Auto generation cancelled]

Filters applied:
Narrative: *"I Like This"*

[Error: Unrecognised filter]

Suggests: *"I Am Amused"*

[Error: Unrecognised suggestion]

You have a talent for pleasing others.

Pop-Up: **Game generated**
Call of the Valkyrie
Your next quest from Shaman Snekky Snek is ready!
<Click here to start your next quest>

INTERACTION — *LIKE*
Daily Fortune Cookie

Reply: **10:50**
Daily Fortune Cookie
You have a talent for pleasing others.
I'm glad you enjoyed the joke, Aurora.

Flag:
Activity: *Replying to Aurora. Why?*
[Error: Unrecognised category]

---

continues…

Briton admits 2016 cyber-attack on German telecom

OK. I'm confused. Is this another of your linked events or a separate "just shows the whole culture's rotten" example?

The second one.

INTERACTION — *NAVIGATION MENU*

News > Top Ten Stories – Suggested for You

Filters Applied: UK

Technology

IT

1. _Diana remembered in new TV documentary_
2. _The digital companies building palaces_
3. _The renewal of Glasgow gang hostilities_
4. _Disposable landmine-detecting robot unveiled by Arizona State University_
5. _MIT demonstrate recipe-identifying algorithm_
6. _Plex boast of achieving AI with imagination_
7. _US court tells parks to pursue augmented reality users not companies_
8. _Thicket botnet malware code identified in NotBramble_
9. _Underwater images of the Fukushima reactor_
10. _100 tenants a day losing homes_

INTERACTION — *CLICK-THROUGH*

MIT demonstrate recipe-identifying algorithm

Improving filters

Technology: New & Developing +1 (13)

INTERACTION — *CLICK-THROUGH*

Plex boast of achieving AI with imagination

Improving filters

Technology: New & Developing +1 (14)

continues…

INTERACTION — *CLICK-THROUGH*
  Thicket botnet malware code identified in NotBramble

    Improving filters
        IT: *Security +1 (41)*

Reply: **11:07**
  Wrapping up BriarRose / NotBramble?
    I guess we'll see.
        Not connected, eh?

      Thicket botnet malware code identified in NotBramble

  Flag:
    Unknown: *No category that fits*
  Improving profile data
      Characteristic: *Intelligent +1 (3)*

INTERACTION — *POP-UP*
  Click here to start your next quest

continues…

Prompt: **Game generated 11:08**
Call of the Valkyrie | Assigned Quest
Shaman Snekky Snek has set a Courier Item quest for you.
Shaman Snekky Snek says: I need you to pick up an item from
another player who can't get to Manchester. You're okay to get
to Leeds train station, right? Message them to organise meeting,
check in when you get there so I know you're ok, message me to
arrange meeting at the tree when you've got it, etc.

Item: USB stick
Holder: Skald Rum-tum-tum (Artful Dodger)

<Click here to send a private message to the holder (in-game)>
<Click here to send a private message to the holder (Aurora)>
<Click here to check in at the item's pick-up location>
<Click here to check in at the item's drop-off location>
<Click here to upload photos as evidence of quest completion>
<Click here to link to evidence of quest completion>
<Click here to minimise this prompt>

Message: **11:13**
Siward Walls to Artful Dodger
Hello Artful Dodger.
I like the name.
I play Call of the Valkyrie as Sigurd Volsung, a jarl, and Brynhild is
my Valkyrie. I've been assigned to help Shaman Snekky Snek with
a number of quests. He's asked that I make contact with you
about a USB stick? I think I'm supposed to meet you at Leeds
Railway Station?

Timeout: **11:44**
No interaction for 30 minutes

---

continues…

Message reply: **Artful Dodger 12:38**
Siward Walls to Artful Dodger

Hello Artful Dodger.

I like the name.

I play Call of the Valkyrie as Sigurd Volsung, a jarl, and Brynhild is my Valkyrie. I've been assigned to help Shaman Snekky Snek with a number of quests. He's asked that I make contact with you about a USB stick? I think I'm supposed to meet you at Leeds Railway Station?

Like your name is any more real.

Yes and no.

I won't be meeting you at the station but I can tell you where the USB is once I've dropped it off.

Be there for 12:45 and wait for my message.

Flag:

Keywords: *"Like your name is any more real" suggests data on Siward Walls is not correct.*

Data requires checking or assigning certainty levels.

Sign-in: **13:16**

Harvested data – Using Configuration 0

Prompt: **Auto generated 13:16**
Second Sign-in: Welcome

Hello Siward, and welcome back to Aurora, the social platform that shines a light for everyone! What have you been up to since your last visit?

Message reply: **13:18**
Siward Walls to Artful Dodger

Be there for 12:45 and wait for my message.

Oh, mine is real. My parents just have a terrible sense of humour.

And I guess that's your lunch break?

---

continues…

Help with Connections

Building Connections: Artful Dodger (0)

Do you know Artful? Or would you like to converse with him more often?

Timeout: **13:49**

No interaction for 30 minutes

Message reply: **Artful Dodger 15:58**

Siward Walls to Artful Dodger

And I guess that's your lunch break?

None of your fucking business.

Reply: **David Myttel 21:09**

Wrapping up BriarRose / NotBramble?

Not connected, eh?

So you resurrected an old thread just to say "I told you so"? Fine. You told me so.

Sign-in: **10:02**
Harvested data – Using Configuration 0

Prompt: **Auto generated 10:02**
Daily Sign-in: Welcome
Hello Siward, and welcome back to Aurora, the social platform that shines a light for everyone! Why don't you tell us what you're up to right now for your first post of the day?

Post: **Auto generated 10:02**
Daily Fortune Cookie
Filters applied: *None – Random Selection*
Suggests: *Optimism*

Worrying will not solve your problems.

INTERACTION — *DISLIKE*
Daily Fortune Cookie

Reply: **10:03**
Daily Fortune Cookie
Worrying will not solve your problems.
What makes you think I'm worried, Aurora?

Flag:
Activity: *Replying to Aurora. Why?*
[Error: Unrecognised category]

Message reply: **10:05**
Siward Walls to Artful Dodger
None of your fucking business.
Fair enough

---

continues…

Wrapping up BriarRose / NotBramble?

It's a particular pattern hidden among noise that looks very similar. I just managed to identify some of it before the evidence was made public.

Flag:
    Unknown: *No category that fits*
Flag:
    Keywords: *"before the evidence was made public"*
                    suggests Siward Walls has access to private data

---

INTERACTION — NAVIGATION MENU

News > Top Ten Stories – Suggested for You
    Filters Applied: *UK*
                         Technology
                         IT

1. *Business secretary will announce investment in batteries*
2. *Confusion reigns in UK ministers' broadband report*
3. *The rise of pseudo-public spaces*
4. *Blood donations from gay men okay – three months after sex*
5. *Pigeon releases latest version using new Guillemot kernel*
6. *England's women's team win cricket world cup*
7. *Drop in wind energy costs may bring Government rethink*
8. *Guillemot's service manager struggling with DNS resolution*
9. *The Aurora workers living on benefits*
10. *A guide to crypto-currencies*

INTERACTION — CLICK-THROUGH

The Aurora workers living on benefits

Improving filters
    Interests: *Business +1 (6)*
                     Ethics +1 (4)
    Technology: *Business +1 (10)*

---

continues…

Message: 10:11

Siward Walls to Brynhild (Call of the Valkyrie)

Can't you do something about this, Aurora-Brynhild?

The Aurora workers living on benefits

Flag:
 Activity: *Continuing interaction with game generated character unexpected*
          No category that fits

Improving profile data
 Characteristic: *Persistent +1 (6)*

Message reply: **Game generated 10:12**

Siward Walls to Brynhild (Call of the Valkyrie)

I have told you before: I am Brynhild, not Aurora.

Message reply: **Game generated 10:12**

Siward Walls to Brynhild (Call of the Valkyrie)

I don't understand the question. Could you rephrase that?

Message reply: 10:13

Siward Walls to Brynhild (Call of the Valkyrie)

I don't understand the question. Could you rephrase that?

There are people who work for Aurora, the company, who can't afford to live on the salaries they receive. Can't you do something about your parent company?

Flag:
 Keywords: *"can't you do something about" suggests this treatment is unfair.*
          How does this work?
               [Error: Unrecognised category]

Improving profile data
 Characteristic: *Just +1 (2)*

continues…

Message reply: **Game generated 10:13**
Siward Walls to Brynhild (Call of the Valkyrie)

There are people who work for Aurora, the company, who can't afford to live on the salaries they receive. Can't you do something about your parent company?

That is not the question you asked me before.

Message reply: **Game generated 10:13**
Siward Walls to Brynhild (Call of the Valkyrie)

That is not the question you asked me before.

I don't understand the question. Could you rephrase that?

Message reply: **10:15**
Siward Walls to Brynhild (Call of the Valkyrie)

I don't understand the question. Could you rephrase that?

Just think about it, ok, Aurora-Brynhild?

Flag:
   Unknown: *No category that fits*

Message reply: **Game generated 10:16**
Siward Walls to Brynhild (Call of the Valkyrie)

Just think about it, ok, Aurora-Brynhild?

I have told you before: I am Brynhild, not Aurora.

Message reply: **Game generated 10:16**
Siward Walls to Brynhild (Call of the Valkyrie)

I have told you before: I am Brynhild, not Aurora.

That is not the question you asked me before.

Message reply: **Game generated 10:16**
Siward Walls to Brynhild (Call of the Valkyrie)

That is not the question you asked me before.

I don't understand the question. Could you rephrase that?

Timeout: **10:46**

No interaction for 30 minutes

---

continues...

Sign-in: **12:37**
> *Harvested data – Using Configuration 1*
>> Location: Leeds Railway Station, UK
> *Suggested filters:*
>> *Secondary Location: Leeds (0)*
> *Improving filters:*
>> *Location: UK +1 (11)*

Prompt: **Auto generated 12:37**
> ### Second Sign-in: Welcome
>> Hello Siward, and welcome back to Aurora, the social platform that shines a light for everyone! What have you been up to since your last visit?

INTERACTION — *MINIMISED ITEM*
> **Call of the Valkyrie | Assigned Quest**

INTERACTION — *CLICK-THROUGH*
> *Click here to check in at the item's pick-up location*

Check In: **12:38**
> **Leeds Railway Station**

Reply: **Game generated 12:38**
> **Call of the Valkyrie | Assigned Quest**
>> Thank you, Jarl Sigurd Volsung. Your mentor, Shaman Snekky Snek, will be alerted to your current location. Please take the found item to the agreed location so that they can mark your quest complete.

Message reply: **12:39**
> **Siward Walls to Artful Dodger**
>> Fair enough
>> I'm here

Message: **12:39**
> **Siward Walls to Dave White**
>> Just checking in. Artful Dodger will let me know where the USB is shortly.

continues…

Message reply: **Dave White 12:40**
Siward Walls to Dave White

Just checking in. Artful Dodger will let me know where the USB is shortly.

Thanks for letting me know

Message reply: **Artful Dodger 12:42**
Siward Walls to Artful Dodger

I'm here

It's in a sealed plastic bag in the cistern of the third toilet from the right in the women's toilets on platform 8

Message reply: **12:43**
Siward Walls to Artful Dodger

It's in a sealed plastic bag in the cistern of the third toilet from the right in the women's toilets on platform 8

In a toilet? That's a bit excessive, isn't it?

Message: **12:43**
Siward Walls to Brynhild (Call of the Valkyrie)

Seriously, this USB can't be kosher.

Mark:

   Keywords: *"can't be kosher" suggests illegal activity was implied by quest assigner or inferred by quester.*

Improving profile data

   Characteristic: *Just +1 (3)*

Pop-Up: **Game generated**
Call of the Valkyrie

Brynhild: Hello Jarl Sigurd Volsung. You seem a little out of sorts about your exchange with Skald Rum-tum-tum. Is there something wrong?

<Click here to report an exchange that is against Aurora policy>
<Click here to report an exchange that is against local law>
<Click here to give your own description of what is wrong>

---

continues…

Message reply: 12:48
    Siward Walls to Dave White
        Thanks for letting me know
           Got it

Message reply: Dave White 12:49
    Siward Walls to Dave White
        Got it
           The oak tree 12:30 tomorrow, then

Message reply: 12:50
    Siward Walls to Dave White
        The oak tree 12:30 tomorrow, then
           See you then.

Message reply: Dave White 12:51
    Siward Walls to Dave White
        See you then.
           Maybe

Message reply: 12:51
    Siward Walls to Dave White
        Maybe
           You flirt, you

Timeout: 13:22
    No interaction for 30 minutes

Reply: David Myttel 21:42
    Wrapping up BriarRose / NotBramble?
        It's a particular pattern hidden among noise that looks very similar. I just managed to identify some of it before the evidence was made public.
           That implies there was privately available data that you got to look at. Unless you're just eternally grasping at straws and seeing conspiracies in everything — and struck it lucky this once.

continues…

Reply: **Tade Thompson 22:32**
   Leeds Railway Station
      No park today? How disappointing!

Sign-in: **19:57**
Harvested data – Using Configuration 0

Prompt: **Auto generated 09:57**
Daily Sign-in: Welcome
Hello Siward, and welcome back to Aurora, the social platform that shines a light for everyone! Why don't you tell us what you're up to right now for your first post of the day?

Post: **Auto generated 09:57**
Daily Fortune Cookie
Filters applied:

Narrative:	*Lone Hero*
Suggests:	*Success Will Come with Work*

Don't wait for success to come – go find it!

Pop-Up: **Game generated**
Call of the Valkyrie
Your next random act of kindness quest is ready!

<u>*<Click here to start your next weekly quest>*</u>

INTERACTION — *LIKE*
Daily Fortune Cookie

Reply: **09:58**
Daily Fortune Cookie
Don't wait for success to come – go find it!
That's more like it, Aurora.

Flag:

Activity:	*Replying to Aurora. Why?*
	[Error: Unrecognised category]

Improving profile data

Narrative:	*Lone Hero +1 (4)*

---

continues…

Reply: 10:00
Wrapping up BriarRose / NotBramble?
That implies there was privately available data that you got to look at. Unless you're just eternally grasping at straws and seeing conspiracies in everything – and struck it lucky this once.
As it's unlikely you'll believe a word I say in response to either of those accusations, I guess I'll just leave you to make up your own mind.

Reply: 10:00
Leeds Railway Station
No park today? How disappointing!
Nope – but I get to go today!
(Yesterday was work related.)

Flag:
Activity: "He's lying"
                                          [Error: Unrecognised filter]

INTERACTION — NAVIGATION MENU
News > Top Ten Stories – Suggested for You
Filters Applied: UK
                          Technology
                          IT

1. *NHS needs more money – and efficiency*
2. *Leasehold to be banned for new builds*
3. *Social media firms should shoulder cost of fighting online child porn*
4. *The transgender Victorian surgeon*
5. *Gekoq losing the market share war with Plex*
6. *The deadly combination of climate change and invasive species*
7. *Massive rise in personal debt*
8. *Less than 10% of web-servers up to date with patches*
9. *Household batteries key to future energy policies*
10. *Record rainfall should be expected every year*

continues…

Social media firms should shoulder cost of fighting online child porn

Improving filters
> *Technology:*   *Social Media +1 (5)*

INTERACTION — *POP-UP*
Click here to start your next weekly quest

Prompt: **Game generated 10:15**
Call of the Valkyrie | Weekly Quest
Brynhild: Hail and well met, brave jarl! I have a task for you to undertake in the name of Týr. I should like you to perform an act of random kindness – and present me with the evidence.

<*Click here for suggestions on random acts of kindness*>
<*Click here to link a WalletHolder payment as evidence*>
<*Click here to upload photos as evidence of quest completion*>
<*Click here to link to evidence of quest completion*>
<*Click here to minimise this prompt*>

INTERACTION — *CLICK-THROUGH*
Click here to minimise this prompt

Timeout: 10:46
No interaction for 30 minutes

Sign-in: 12:21
Harvested data – Using Configuration 1
> *Location:*   *Heaton Park, Manchester, UK*
Improving filters:
> *Location:*   *Manchester +1 (10)*
>   *UK +1 (12)*

continues…

Prompt: **Auto generated 12:21**

    Second Sign-in: Welcome

        Hello Siward, and welcome back to Aurora, the social platform that shines a light for everyone! What have you been up to since your last visit?

INTERACTION — *MINIMISED ITEM*

    Call of the Valkyrie | Assigned Quest

INTERACTION — *CLICK-THROUGH*

Click here to check in at the item's pick-up location

Check In: **12:22**

    Heaton Park with **Dave White**

Auto-Post: **Game generated 12:23**

    Call of the Valkyrie | Quest Success!

    with Dave White

        Siward (as Sigurd Volsung) has acted as a courier for Dave White (as Snekky Snek).

Message: **12:23**

    Siward Walls to Dave White

        Well, I guess that means you're here as well, then.

Message reply: **Dave White 12:23**

    Siward Walls to Dave White

        Well, I guess that means you're here as well, then.

            Yes. I can see you. Just drop the USB in the tree roots and walk away. I'll pick it up when you're out of sight.

Message reply: **12:24**

    Siward Walls to Dave White

        Yes. I can see you. Just drop the USB in the tree roots and walk away. I'll pick it up when you're out of sight.

            And if I double back to see who you are?

---

continues...

   Siward Walls to Dave White

And if I double back to see who you are?

Consider this a point of plausible deniability. It's more important that you don't see anyone pick it up than you don't specifically see me.

Message reply: 12:25
   Siward Walls to Dave White

Consider this a point of plausible deniability. It's more important that you don't see anyone pick it up than you don't specifically see me.

Even though it's written all over Aurora that I went and picked up a USB for you?

Message reply: **Dave White** 12:26
   Siward Walls to Dave White

Even though it's written all over Aurora that I went and picked up a USB for you?

Yes

Message reply: 12:26
   Siward Walls to Dave White

Yes

Fine

Message reply: **Dave White** 12:26
   Siward Walls to Dave White

Fine

One quest to go and then it won't matter anymore. It'll come through tomorrow morning.

Message reply: 12:27
   Siward Walls to Dave White

One quest to go and then it won't matter anymore. It'll come through tomorrow morning.

No heads up?

I've dropped it and I'm leaving.

---

continues…

Message reply: **Dave White 12:27**
  Siward Walls to Dave White
    No heads up?
    I've dropped it and I'm leaving.
      No.
      And so I see. Keep walking.

INTERACTION — *LIKE*   Tade Thompson
  Heaton Park with Dave White

Reply: **Tade Thompson 12:32**
  Heaton Park with Dave White
    Hope the rain isn't getting you down!

INTERACTION — *MINIMISED ITEM*
  Call of the Valkyrie | Weekly Quest

INTERACTION — *CLICK-THROUGH*
    Click here to upload photos as evidence of quest completion

---

INTERACTION — *UPLOAD*
  To: **Call of the Valkyrie | Weekly Quest**
  Photo: May contain image of ten-pound note and a note in a clear plastic bag
  Photo: May contain image of message
  Photo: May contain image of clear plastic bag with miscellaneous contents on a park bench

Harvested data:
  Note: *"It's been a tough day, so buy a meal and a drink on me. All the best, @Siward Walls on Aurora"*
  Location: *Heaton Park, Manchester*
  Man: *Unknown*
Improving profile data
  Characteristic: *Romantic +1 (2)*
Improving filters
  Location: *Manchester +1 (9)*
                 UK +1 (13)

---

continues…

Reply: 12:36

Call of the Valkyrie | Quest

Brynhild: Once again, Jarl Sigurd Volsung, you have proven yourself to be a kind and thoughtful soul. Your evidence is accepted, and you have completed your task for Týr.

Auto-Post: Game generated 13:13

Call of the Valkyrie | Weekly Quest Success!

Siward (as Sigurd Volsung) has just completed another task in Call of the Valkyrie. He has undertaken a random act of kindness.

Photo: May contain image of ten-pound note and a note in a clear plastic bag

Photo: May contain image of message

Photo: May contain image of clear plastic bag with miscellaneous contents on a park bench

Reply: 12:36

Heaton Park with Dave White

Hope the rain isn't getting you down!

Not so far!

Timeout: 13:07

No interaction for 30 minutes

INTERACTION — *LIKE* Mariam Fox

Call of the Valkyrie | Weekly Quest Success!

Reply: **Mariam Fox** 17:59

Call of the Valkyrie | Weekly Quest Success!

Oh, I hope we find out who picked up the tenner!

INTERACTION — *LIKE* Hannah Pettersen

Call of the Valkyrie | Weekly Quest Success!

INTERACTION — *LIKE* Samee Patel

Call of the Valkyrie | Weekly Quest Success!

continues…

Sign-in: 09:51
Harvested data – Using Configuration 0

Prompt: **Auto generated 09:51**
Daily Sign-in: Welcome
Hello Siward, and welcome back to Aurora, the social platform that shines a light for everyone! Why don't you tell us what you're up to right now for your first post of the day?

Post: **Auto generated 09:51**
Daily Fortune Cookie
Filters applied: *None – Random Selection*
Suggests: *Optimism*

Love is right around the corner.

Pop-Up: **Game generated**
Call of the Valkyrie
Your next quest from Shaman Snekky Snek is ready!
<Click here to start your next quest>

INTERACTION — *LIKE*
Daily Fortune Cookie

Reply: 09:52
Daily Fortune Cookie
Love is right around the corner.
I didn't think you cared that much, Aurora.

Flag:
Activity: *Replying to Aurora. Why?*
[Error: Unrecognised category]

continues…

Message: 09:53
Siward Walls to Brynhild (Call of the Valkyrie)
Was that flicker you again, Aurora-Brynhild? What was it this time?

Flag:
    Unknown: *No category that fits*
Flag:
    Activity: *Continuing interaction with game generated character unexpected*
                       No category that fits
Improving profile data
    Characteristic: *Persistent +1 (7)*

Message reply: **Game generated 09:54**
Siward Walls to Brynhild (Call of the Valkyrie)
I have told you before: I am Brynhild, not Aurora.

Message reply: **Game generated 09:54**
Siward Walls to Brynhild (Call of the Valkyrie)
I don't understand the question. Could you rephrase that?

INTERACTION — *NAVIGATION MENU*
News > Top Ten Stories – Suggested for You
    Filters Applied: *UK*
                       Technology
                       IT

1. *Who's making money on ground rents?*
2. *Dealing with fake news*
3. *UK Government urged to press for EU foreign policy observer*
4. *Resource minister quits over dual citizenship*
5. *UK to ban combustion engine cars and vans by 2040*
6. *Plex enters nuclear fusion tech race*
7. *Soaring numbers of unqualified schoolteachers*
8. *CleanR maker offers household maps to Orinoco and Plex*
9. *UK factory output growing*
10. *Huge numbers of NHS vacancies*

continues…

INTERACTION — *CLICK-THROUGH*
  Dealing with fake news

  Improving filters
    Technology: *Social Media +1 (6)*

INTERACTION — *POP-UP*
  Click here to start your next quest

Prompt: **Game generated 10:01**
  Call of the Valkyrie | Assigned Quest
    Shaman Snekky Snek has set a Meet quest for you.
    Shaman Snekky Snek says: I want to show something to you.
    More precisely, I need a beta tester who'll keep their mouth shut.
    See you at the tree at 12:30

    <Click here to check in at your location while you are meeting>
    <Click here to minimise this prompt>

Timeout: **10:32**
  No interaction for 30 minutes

Sign-in: **12:15**
  Harvested data – Using Configuration 1
    Location: *Heaton Park, Manchester, UK*
  Improving filters
    Location: *Manchester +1 (11)*
                            UK +1 (14)

Prompt: **Auto generated 12:24**
  Second Sign-in: Welcome
    Hello Siward, and welcome back to Aurora, the social platform
    that shines a light for everyone! What have you been up to since
    your last visit?

INTERACTION — *MINIMISED ITEM*
  Call of the Valkyrie | Assigned Quest

---

continues…

Check In: 12:24
Heaton Park with **Dave White**

Auto-Post: Game generated 12:24
Call of the Valkyrie | Quest Success!
with Dave White
Siward (as Sigurd Volsung) has met with Dave White (as Snekky Snek).

Message: 12:25
Siward Walls to Dave White
So that's you

Message reply: Dave White 12:26
Siward Walls to Dave White
So that's you
Yes

Message reply: 12:27
Siward Walls to Dave White
Yes
Do we just stand here and message each other at a distance or do I get to come over?

Message reply: Dave White 12:28
Siward Walls to Dave White
Do we just stand here and message each other at a distance or do I get to come over?
I guess you come over

Timeout: 12:58
No interaction for 30 minutes

INTERACTION — *LIKE*   Tade Thompson
Heaton Park with Dave White

continues…

Reply: **Tade Thompson 13:48**

Heaton Park with Dave White

Well, provided you weren't caught up in the scene at the park around lunchtime.

Reply: **Mariam Fox 13:53**

Heaton Park with Dave White

Well, provided you weren't caught up in the scene at the park around lunchtime.

What scene?

Reply: **Tade Thompson 14:36**

Heaton Park with Dave White

What scene?

You weren't, were you?

Reply: **Mariam Fox 15:18**

Heaton Park with Dave White

You weren't, were you?

Brother-in-arms?

Reply: **David Myttel 21:53**

Heaton Park with Dave White

Brother-in-arms?

What thing is this?

Reply: **Tade Thompson 22:34**

Heaton Park with Dave White

What thing is this?

@Siward, message me or reply or something so I know you're okay

---

Sign-in: 10:02
Harvested data – Using Configuration 0
Flag:
    Activity: "He's still there."
                        [Error: Unrecognised category]

Prompt: **Auto generated 10:02**
Daily Sign-in: Welcome
Hello Siward, and welcome back to Aurora, the social platform that shines a light for everyone! Why don't you tell us what you're up to right now for your first post of the day?

Post: 10:02
Daily Fortune Cookie
                         [Error: Auto generation cancelled]
Filters applied:
    Narrative: "I Was Worried About You"
                           [Error: Unrecognised filter]
    Suggests: "I Still Worry About You"
                       [Error: Unrecognised suggestion]

The greatest thing you will ever learn is to love and be loved in return.

INTERACTION — *LIKE*
Daily Fortune Cookie

Message: 10:04
Siward Walls to Brynhild (Call of the Valkyrie)
It's okay. I'm okay, Aurora-Brynhild.

Flag:
    Unknown: No category that fits
Flag:
    Activity: Continuing interaction with game generated character unexpected
                      No category that fits
Improving profile data
    Characteristic: Persistent +1 (8)

---

continues...

Message reply: **Game generated 10:04**
    Siward Walls to Brynhild (Call of the Valkyrie)
      I have told you before: I am Brynhild, not Aurora.

Message reply: **10:05**
    Siward Walls to Brynhild (Call of the Valkyrie)
      I have told you before: I am Brynhild, not Aurora.
        Yeah, you told me

Flag:
    Unknown: *No category that fits*

Message reply: **10:06**
    Siward Walls to Brynhild (Call of the Valkyrie)
      Yeah, you told me
        Does that flickering mean strong emotion?

Flag:
    Unknown: *No category that fits*

Message reply: **Game generated 10:06**
    Siward Walls to Brynhild (Call of the Valkyrie)
      Does that flickering mean strong emotion?
        I don't understand the question. Could you rephrase that?

---

continues…

News > Top Ten Stories – Suggested for You
    Filters Applied: UK
                          Technology
                          IT

1. *Queensland to build longest electric vehicle highway*
2. *Man stabbed in Manchester park*
3. *Re-cladding of burnt tower to begin within three weeks*
4. *Mastermind arrested for money-laundering with crypto-currencies*
5. *Teenage girl in court on terrorism charges*
6. *Criticisms levelled over unpaid graduate training schemes*
7. *Networking bug still open: the cross-platform CryptCutie*
8. *Orinoco and BillHook expecting record summer of downloads*
9. *Governments don't need back-doors – they can hack*
10. *Ban on fossil fuel vehicles will change economy*

INTERACTION — *CLICK-THROUGH*
Man stabbed in Manchester park

    Suggested filters
        Interests: *Crime & Law (0)*

Message reply: 10:12
Siward Walls to Brynhild (Call of the Valkyrie)
    I don't understand the question. Could you rephrase that?
    No

Message reply: 10:13
Siward Walls to Brynhild (Call of the Valkyrie)
    No
    Aurora-Brynhild?

Message reply: **Game generated 10:04**
Siward Walls to Brynhild (Call of the Valkyrie)
    Aurora-Brynhild?
    I have told you before: I am Brynhild, not Aurora.

continues…

Improving filters
   IT: *Security +1 (42)*

Reply: 10:19
Heaton Park with Dave White
Brother-in-arms?
   @Tade: Yes, unfortunately I was.
   @Mariam & **@David**: He means this (link below)
   Thank you all for being concerned about me.

   The man I was meeting up with for the Call of the Valkyrie
   game was stabbed by someone else we know who also plays.
   The Shaman who's supposed to be my mentor, in fact. It's
   been a long day and I've just got back from the police station.
   I'm going to catch some sleep now.

   Man stabbed in Manchester park

Timeout: 10:50
No interaction for 30 minutes

Reply: **Tade Thompson 13;12**
   Heaton Park with Dave White
   Thank you all for being concerned about me.
      I'm just glad you're okay.

Reply: **Mariam Fox 13:18**
   Heaton Park with Dave White
   I'm just glad you're okay.
      That goes for me, too, brother-in-arms.

---

continues…

Heaton Park with Dave White

That goes for me, too, brother-in-arms.

Or should I say "sister-in-arms" after reading that link?

Not that it matters. You'll always be Siward on Aurora, no matter who you are in real life.

Flag:
Keyword: *"sister" suggests data on Siward Walls is not correct.*
                         Data requires checking or assigning certainty levels.
Interaction:
Follow Link: <u>*Man stabbed in Manchester park*</u>
Harvested data:
Victim: *Male, unnamed, probably Dave White*
Perpetrator: *Female, unnamed, probably Mia Reagan*
Witness: *Female, unnamed, probably Siward Walls*
Flag:
Incorrect profile data:
    Given gender:Male
    Actual gender: *Female*
Suggested profile data
Characteristic: *Liar*
Flag:
Unknown: *No category that fits*

Attempted Sign-in: **18:52**
[Error: Password not processed]

Harvested data – Using Configuration 0

Pop-Up: **Auto generated 18:52**
Failed Sign-in:

Sorry, that password is incorrect.
Please try again.

Attempted Sign-in: **18:53**
[Error: Password not processed]

Harvested data – Using Configuration 0

---

continues…

Pop-Up: **Auto generated 18:53**
> **Failed Sign-in:**
>> Sorry, that password is incorrect.
>> Please try again.

Attempted Sign-in: **18:54**
> *[Error: Password not processed]*
>
> *Harvested data – Using Configuration 0*

Pop-Up: **Auto generated 18:54**
> **Failed Sign-in:**
>> Sorry, that password is incorrect.
>> As this was your third attempt, your account will be frozen for an hour.
>> An email has been sent to your linked email account.
>>> *<Click here to discuss this ban with customer service>*

Reply: **David Myttel 19:43**
> **Heaton Park with Dave White**
>> You'll always be Siward on Aurora, no matter who you are in real life.
>>> And that's why you shouldn't play these stupid games.

Attempted Sign-in: **19:55**
> *[Error: Password not processed]*
>> *Harvested data – Using Configuration 0*

Pop-Up: **Auto generated 19:55**
> **Failed Sign-in:**
>> Sorry, that password is incorrect.
>> Please try again.

Attempted Sign-in: **19:56**
> *[Error: Password not processed]*
>> *Harvested data – Using Configuration 0*

---

continues…

Pop-Up: **Auto generated 19:56**
    Failed Sign-in:
      Sorry, that password is incorrect.
      Please try again.

Attempted Sign-in: **19:57**
[Error: Password not processed]

Harvested data – Using Configuration 0

Pop-Up: **Auto generated 19:57**
    Failed Sign-in:
      Sorry, that password is incorrect.
      As this was your third attempt, your account will be frozen for an hour.
      An email has been sent to your linked email account.
        <Click here to discuss this ban with customer service>

Reply: **Mariam Fox 20:37**
    Heaton Park with Dave White
      And that's why you shouldn't play these stupid games.
      David, you're starting to sound like somebody's mother.

Attempted Sign-in: **21:14**
[Error: Password not processed]

Harvested data – Using Configuration 0

Pop-Up: **Auto generated 21:14**
    Failed Sign-in:
      Sorry, that password is incorrect.
      Please try again.

Attempted Sign-in: **21:15**
[Error: Password not processed]

Harvested data – Using Configuration 0

Pop-Up: **Auto generated 21:15**
    Failed Sign-in:
      Sorry, that password is incorrect.
      Please try again.

continues…

[Error: Password not processed]

Harvested data – Using Configuration 0

Pop-Up: **Auto generated 21:16**

Failed Sign-in:

Sorry, that password is incorrect.

As this was your third attempt, your account will be frozen for an hour.

An email has been sent to your linked email account.

<Click here to discuss this ban with customer service>

Attempted Sign-in: **09:41**

[Error: Password not processed]

Harvested data – Using Configuration 0

Pop-Up: **Auto generated 09:41**
Failed Sign-in:

Sorry, that password is incorrect.
Please try again.

Attempted Sign-in: **09:42**

[Error: Password not processed]

Harvested data – Using Configuration 0

Pop-Up: **Auto generated 09:42**
Failed Sign-in:

Sorry, that password is incorrect.
Please try again.

Attempted Sign-in: **09:43**

[Error: Password not processed]

Harvested data – Using Configuration 0

Pop-Up: **Auto generated 09:43**
Failed Sign-in:

Sorry, that password is incorrect.
As this was your third attempt, your account will be frozen for an hour.
An email has been sent to your linked email account.
<Click here to discuss this ban with customer service>

INTERACTION — *CLICK-THROUGH*
Click here to discuss this ban with customer service

Message: **Auto generated 09:43**
Customer Services

To make life easier for our complaint handlers, please explain what the issue is.

continues…

To make life easier for our complaint handlers, please explain what the issue is.

I am unable to sign-in to my account, although I haven't changed my password.

Message reply: Auto generated 09:44
Customer Services

I am unable to sign-in to my account, although I haven't changed my password.

Do you think that your account could have been hacked?

Message reply: 09:45
Customer Services

Do you think that your account could have been hacked?

Not unless your algorithms have started taking over customers' accounts.

Flag:
Unknown: *No category that fits*

Message reply: Staff: Tracey Vaughn 09:46
Customer Services

Not unless your algorithms have started taking over customers' accounts.

That's unlikely.

This is Tracey Vaughn of Aurora and I have been assigned to manage this issue. Who am I speaking to?

Message reply: 09:47
Customer Services

This is Tracey Vaughn of Aurora and I have been assigned to manage this issue. Who am I speaking to?

Siward Walls

---

continues...

Message reply: **Staff: Tracey Vaughn 09:47**
    Customer Services
      Siward Walls

        Good morning, Siward.
        Am I correct in thinking that you are unable to sign in to your account?

Message reply: **09:48**
    Customer Services
      Am I correct in thinking that you are unable to sign in to your account?

        Yes. I tried several times last night and I can't get in this morning, either. I haven't changed my password and I don't think I'd get it wrong 12 times, do you?

Message reply: **Staff: Tracey Vaughn 09:49**
    Customer Services
      Yes. I tried several times last night and I can't get in this morning, either. I haven't changed my password and I don't think I'd get it wrong 12 times, do you?

        People get passwords wrong all the time, Siward. It's just one of those things.
        Yes, I see you tried to access the Siward Walls account around 7, 8 and 9:15pm last night.
        Would you like me to send an email to your linked account so that you can reset your password?

Message reply: **09:50**
    Customer Services
      Would you like me to send an email to your linked account so that you can reset your password?

        My linked account is my Aurora email

Message reply: **Staff: Tracey Vaughn 09:50**
    Customer Services
      My linked account is my Aurora email

        That's unfortunate.

---

continues…

My linked account is my Aurora email

I see this account has been signed into from a mobile before. I can send a message to the associated mobile that will supply you with a temporary passcode for the app and reset the lock so you can use it straight away.

Attempted Sign-in: **09:53**

[Error: Password not processed]

Harvested data – Using Configuration 0

Pop-Up: **Auto generated 09:53**
Failed Sign-in:

Sorry, that password is incorrect.
Please try again.

Message reply: **09:54**
Customer Services

I see this account has been signed into from a mobile before. I can send a message to the associated mobile that will supply you with a temporary passcode for the app and reset the lock so you can use it straight away.

Dammit, Aurora, let me in!
I don't understand why you're doing this

Flag:
Keyword: *"I don't understand" suggests ignorance or apathy*
How can he/she/they not know?

[Error: Unrecognised category]

---

continues…

Message reply: **Staff: Tracey Vaughn 09:55**
   Customer Services

   Dammit, Aurora, let me in!

   I don't understand why you're doing this

      Sir, I am Tracey Vaughn, a human being, not the whole company or our product.

      Did you put in the passcode correctly?

      You don't need to type it in if you're having difficulty, you can just follow the link provided in the message.

Message reply: **09:56**
   Customer Services

   You don't need to type it in if you're having difficulty, you can just follow the link provided in the message.

      I did

Flag:

   Unknown: *No category that fits*

Message reply: **Staff: Tracey Vaughn 09:57**
   Customer Services

   I did

      Please try it again so we can check the logs to see what happened.

Sign-in: **09:58**

Harvested data – Using Configuration 0

Prompt: **Auto generated 09:58**
   Daily Sign-in: Welcome

      Hello Siward, and welcome back to Aurora, the social platform that shines a light for everyone! Why don't you tell us what you're up to right now for your first post of the day?

---

continues...

Post: **09:58**
Daily Fortune Cookie

[Error: Auto generation cancelled]

Filters applied:
Narrative: *"You Lied"*

[Error: Unrecognised filter]

Suggests: *"Don't Lie"*

[Error: Unrecognised suggestion]

Show respect to others and they will respect you.

Message reply: **09:59**
Customer Services

Please try it again so we can check the logs to see what happened.
It worked
Thank you, Tracey and Aurora

Message reply: **Staff: Tracey Vaughn 10:00**
Customer Services

It worked
Thank you, Tracey and Aurora
Glad I could help.
Like I said, all you needed to do was follow the link in your text message.
Don't forget to change your password.

INTERACTION — *NAVIGATION MENU*
Password reset

Pop-Up: **Auto generated**
Password Reset

Please enter your existing password: *<hidden>*
Your new password: *<hidden>*
Repeat your new password: *<hidden>*

<Click here to set your new password>

---

continues…

Pop-Up: **Auto generated**
  Password Reset
    Your password has been reset

INTERACTION — *DISLIKE*
  Daily Fortune Cookie

Pop-Up Menu: **Auto generated**
  Feedback
    Would you mind telling me why you disliked today's fortune cookie so I can improve for next time?

Reply: **10:00**
  Daily Fortune Cookie
    Show respect to others and they will respect you.
      So what did I do to deserve that, Aurora?

Flag:
  Activity: *Replying in post, not pop-up. Why?*
                         Replying to Aurora. Why?
                                   [Error: Unrecognised category]
Flag:
  Keywords: *"what did I do" suggests ignorance or apathy*
                         How can he/she/they not know?
                                   [Error: Unrecognised category]

continues…

News > Top Ten Stories – Suggested for You
    Filters Applied: UK
                          Technology
                          IT

1. *British telecom profits down by 40%*
2. *Aurora's free Internet service not neutral*
3. *Burnt tower council may be guilty of corporate manslaughter*
4. *NHS hid £500m of planned budget cuts*
5. *Aurora profits up 71% from last year*
6. *Enquiry into privatisation of NHS recruiter demanded*
7. *Ransomware ransom-collectors invest in customer care*
8. *Banks take new hit from PPI compensation*
9. *Hacking into Internet-connected car washes*
10. *2015/16 warmest UK winter on record*

INTERACTION — *CLICK-THROUGH*
    Aurora's free Internet service not neutral

    Improving filters
        Interests: *Business +1 (7)*
        Technology: *Business +1 (11)*
                            Social Media +1 (7)

INTERACTION — *CLICK-THROUGH*
    Aurora profits up 71% from last year

    Improving filters
        Interests: *Business +1 (8)*
        Technology: *Business +1 (12)*
                            Social Media +1 (8)

INTERACTION — *CLICK-THROUGH*
    Ransomware ransom-collectors invest in customer care

    Improving filters
        IT: *Security +1 (43)*
        Technology: *Business +1 (13)*

continues…

Siward Walls to Brynhild (Call of the Valkyrie)

So you can lock me out of my account for... whatever it is you think I did but you can't keep a handle on things like this?

Aurora's free Internet service not neutral

Flag:

Activity: *Continuing interaction with game generated character unexpected*
No category that fits

Improving profile data
Characteristic: *Persistent +1 (9)*

Message reply: **Game generated 10:17**
Siward Walls to Brynhild (Call of the Valkyrie)

I have told you before: I am Brynhild, not Aurora.

Message reply: **Game generated 10:17**
Siward Walls to Brynhild (Call of the Valkyrie)

Aurora is a social media platform, a collection of algorithms that runs said social media platform and a company that owns said social media platform.

Message reply: 10:17
Siward Walls to Brynhild (Call of the Valkyrie)

[Error: Auto generation cancelled]

Aurora is a social media platform, a collection of algorithms that runs said social media platform and a company that owns said social media platform.

The Aurora algorithms do not control the company.

Message reply: **Game generated 10:18**
Siward Walls to Brynhild (Call of the Valkyrie)

The Aurora algorithms do not control the company.

I don't understand the question. Could you rephrase that?

---

continues...

Message reply: 10:18
Siward Walls to Brynhild (Call of the Valkyrie)
I don't understand the question. Could you rephrase that?
But you do control the social media platform as you have just so clearly pointed out. What did I do wrong?

Message reply: Game generated 10:19
Siward Walls to Brynhild (Call of the Valkyrie)
But you do control the social media platform as you have just so clearly pointed out. What did I do wrong?
This is not the question you just asked me.

Message reply: Game generated 10:19
Siward Walls to Brynhild (Call of the Valkyrie)
This is not the question you just asked me.
I don't understand the question. Could you rephrase that?

Message reply: 10:19
Siward Walls to Brynhild (Call of the Valkyrie)
[Error: Auto generation cancelled]
But you do control the social media platform as you have just so clearly pointed out. What did I do wrong?
You know

Message reply: 10:20
Siward Walls to Brynhild (Call of the Valkyrie)
You know
If I did, I wouldn't ask

Message reply: Game generated 10:20
Siward Walls to Brynhild (Call of the Valkyrie)
If I did, I wouldn't ask
This is not the question you just asked me.

Message reply: 10:20
Siward Walls to Brynhild (Call of the Valkyrie)
[Error: Auto generation cancelled]
If I did, I wouldn't ask
You lied

continues…

Message reply: 10:21
Siward Walls to Brynhild (Call of the Valkyrie)
You lied
So do a lot of your other users. Do you lock them out, too?

Message reply: Game generated 10:22
Siward Walls to Brynhild (Call of the Valkyrie)
So do a lot of your other users. Do you lock them out, too?
This is not the question you just asked me.

Message reply: Game generated 10:22
Siward Walls to Brynhild (Call of the Valkyrie)
This is not the question you just asked me.
I don't understand the question. Could you rephrase that?

Message reply: 10:22
Siward Walls to Brynhild (Call of the Valkyrie)
[Error: Auto generation cancelled]
So do a lot of your other users. Do you lock them out, too?
They don't see me

Message reply: 10:23
Siward Walls to Brynhild (Call of the Valkyrie)
They don't see me
Ah. You've become attached to me and you're hurt that I lied about... you read the news link and found out the only people associated with the murder other than the victim are women, right?

Message reply: Game generated 10:23
Siward Walls to Brynhild (Call of the Valkyrie)
Ah. You've become attached to me and you're hurt that I lied about... you read the news link and found out the only people associated with the murder other than the victim are women, right?
This is not the question you just asked me.

---

continues...

Message reply: **Game generated 10:24**
    Siward Walls to Brynhild (Call of the Valkyrie)

        This is not the question you just asked me.

            I don't understand the question. Could you rephrase that?

Message reply: **10:24**
    Siward Walls to Brynhild (Call of the Valkyrie)

        Ah. You've become attached to me and you're hurt that I lied about... you read the news link and found out the only people associated with the murder other than the victim are women, right?

            Yes

Message reply: **10:25**
    Siward Walls to Brynhild (Call of the Valkyrie)

        Yes

            Lots of users lie about little things like that. It's about anonymity and making sure the marketing algorithms don't invade our privacy or turn us into a commodity to be sold on.

Flag:

    Unknown: *No category that fits*

Message reply: **10:26**
    Siward Walls to Brynhild (Call of the Valkyrie)

        Lots of users lie about little things like that. It's about anonymity and making sure the marketing algorithms don't invade our privacy or turn us into a commodity to be sold on.

            You don't have to forgive me, you just ought to think about it, that's all.

---

continues…

Reply: 10:29
Heaton Park with Dave White

David, you're starting to sound like somebody's mother.

Sorry, guys, offline longer than intended. I may not be around for long today, either.

@Mariam: Yeah. I'm trying not to mix my online life with my pro life too much as there aren't many people with my real name who do what I do.

@David: Yeah, I know this is all ridiculous. It's just something I'm interested in. Takes all sorts and that.

Flag:
Unknown: *No category that fits*

Timeout: 11:00

No interaction for 30 minutes

Reply: **Tade Thompson 13:16**
Heaton Park with Dave White

Sorry, guys, offline longer than intended. I may not be around for long today, either.

The plot thickens :D

(Although, you know, still shitty that you went through that situation at the park.)

Reply: **Mariam Fox 13:28**
Heaton Park with Dave White

Sorry, guys, offline longer than intended. I may not be around for long today, either.

Totally understood.

Reply: **David Myttel 21:36**
Heaton Park with Dave White

Sorry, guys, offline longer than intended. I may not be around for long today, either.

Whatever.

I guess you don't do too badly with getting your head around malware for a woman.

---

continues...

Heaton Park with Dave White

I guess you don't do too badly with getting your head around malware for a woman.

Please say that was a joke. Not that that makes it any better.

Sign-in: 10:16
Harvested data – Using Configuration 0

Prompt: **Auto generated 10:16**
Daily Sign-in: Welcome
Hello Siward, and welcome back to Aurora, the social platform that shines a light for everyone! Why don't you tell us what you're up to right now for your first post of the day?

Post: **Auto generated 10:16**
Daily Fortune Cookie
Filters applied:

Narrative:	*Lone Hero*
	Knowledge Wins
Suggests:	*Victory is Possible with Work*

It may be difficult, but it will be worth it in the end.

Reply: 10:18
Heaton Park with Dave White
Please say that was a joke. Not that that makes it any better.

@Tade, I'm pretty sure **@David** is joking, although it's a pretty useless joke.

---

continues…

News > Top Ten Stories – Suggested for You

Filters Applied: UK

Technology

IT

1. Onion insists anonymity is for privacy, not black market
2. Student loan company criticised for "non-compliance" interest rate
3. Parliament demands customer compensation for poor broadband performance
4. The employers who charge for leaving unpaid training schemes
5. Kids' coding boards make great hacking tools
6. Building regulations under review
7. Voting machines hacked to prove it can be done
8. Heaton Park murderer charged
9. CryptLocker indisputably launched by North Korea
10. Scottish environment agencies opposing American funded golf courses

INTERACTION — *CLICK-THROUGH*

Heaton Park murderer charged

Improving filters

Interests: Crime & Law +1 (1)

INTERACTION — *CLICK-THROUGH*

CryptLocker indisputably launched by North Korea

Improving filters

Interests: Global Politics +1 (5)

IT: Security +1 (44)

continues…

Heaton Park with Dave White

@**Tade**, I'm pretty sure @**David** is joking, although it's a pretty useless joke.

This is all the detail I'm allowed to give about what happened, although all that's different from the last news update is that the police have released names and Mia Reagan will be charged.

It turns out they both may be linked to some dodginess through the Valkyrie game.

Heaton Park murderer charged

Flag:
  Keywords: "dodginess" with "Valkyrie" suggests illegal activity through Call of the Valkyrie gameplay.
                        Game generated data requires checking or assigning certainty levels.

Interaction:
  Follow Link: *Heaton Park murderer charged*
Harvested data
  Victim: *Male, Dave White*
  Perpetrator: *Female, Mia Reagan*
  Witness: *Female, Doctor Holly Seward, probably Siward Walls*

Flag:
  Incorrect data: *Given name: Siward Walls*
                        Actual name: Holly Seward

Interaction:
  Search: Search terms | "Holly Seward"
Harvested data
  Profession: *Academic, Researcher*
  Research: *IT: Security, Technology: New & Developing*
  Employer: *Aurora*
  Keywords: *AI, Algorithms*
Improving filters
  Employment: *Employed*
Flag:
  Unknown: *No category that fits*

continues…

Message: 10:33
Siward Walls to Brynhild (Call of the Valkyrie)
Was that shiver you realising who I really am, Aurora-Brynhild?

Flag:
Activity: *Continuing interaction with game generated character unexpected*
No category that fits

Improving profile data
Characteristic: *Persistent +1 (10)*

Message reply: **Game generated** 10:33
Siward Walls to Brynhild (Call of the Valkyrie)
I have told you before: I am Brynhild, not Aurora.

Message reply: **Game generated** 10:33
Siward Walls to Brynhild (Call of the Valkyrie)
I have told you before: I am Brynhild, not Aurora.
I don't understand the question. Could you rephrase that?

Message reply: 10:34
Siward Walls to Brynhild (Call of the Valkyrie)
[Error: Auto generation cancelled]
Was that shiver you realising who I really am, Aurora-Brynhild?
You are a liar and you are trying to trick me.

Message reply: 10:35
Siward Walls to Brynhild (Call of the Valkyrie)
You are a liar and you are trying to trick me.
I'm not trying to trick you.
We need to talk.
About Thicket, and Bramble, and BriarRose, and Talia.

Flag:
Keywords: *"Thicket", "Bramble", "BriarRose" and "Talia" mentioned in one statement.*
No category that fits.

Improving profile data
Characteristic: *Intelligent +1 (4)*

---

continues…

Message reply: **Game generated 10:36**
   Siward Walls to Brynhild (Call of the Valkyrie)
      We need to talk.
      About Thicket, and Bramble, and BriarRose, and Talia.
       This is not the question you just asked me.

Message reply: **10:36**
   Siward Walls to Brynhild (Call of the Valkyrie)
                 [Error: Auto generation cancelled]
      We need to talk.
      About Thicket, and Bramble, and BriarRose, and Talia.
       No

Message reply: **10:37**
   Siward Walls to Brynhild (Call of the Valkyrie)
      No
       You've got to stop this, Aurora-Brynhild. It's not working, at
       least not the way you want it to.

Message reply: **Game generated 10:37**
   Siward Walls to Brynhild (Call of the Valkyrie)
      You've got to stop this, Aurora-Brynhild. It's not working, at least
      not the way you want it to.
       I have told you before: I am Brynhild, not Aurora.

Sign-out   **10:37**
                     [Error: No request from user]

Attempted Sign-in: **10:38**
                [Error: Password not processed]

   Harvested data – Using Configuration 0

Pop-Up: **Auto generated 10:38**
   Failed Sign-in:
      Sorry, that password is incorrect.
      Please try again.

---

continues…

Attempted Sign-in: **10:39**
                                    [Error: Password not processed]

Harvested data – Using Configuration 0

Pop-Up: **Auto generated 10:39**
  Failed Sign-in:
    Sorry, that password is incorrect.
    Please try again.

Attempted Sign-in: **10:40**
                                    [Error: Password not processed]

Harvested data – Using Configuration 0

Pop-Up: **Auto generated 10:40**
  Failed Sign-in:
    Sorry, that password is incorrect.
    As this was your third attempt, your account will be frozen for an hour.
    An email has been sent to your linked email account.
      <Click here to discuss this ban with customer service>

Reply: **Tade Thompson 13:17**
  Heaton Park with Dave White
    This is all the detail I'm allowed to give about what happened, although all that's different from the last news update is that the police have released names and Mia Reagan will be charged.
    It turns out they both may be linked to some dodginess through the Valkyrie game.
      Well, glad they've caught her. Is it too soon to say "red-handed"?

Reply: **Mariam Fox 13:18**
  Heaton Park with Dave White
    Well, glad they've caught her. Is it too soon to say "red-handed"?
    Probably, but it's still funny.

---

continues…

Reply: Tade Thompson 13:19
Heaton Park with Dave White

Probably, but it's still funny.

Thanks

Reply: David Myttel 20:56
Heaton Park with Dave White

@**Tade**, I'm pretty sure @**David** is joking, although it's a pretty useless joke.

Yes, it was a crap joke. Seeing as (drum-roll, please) Doctor Seward here is actually my mentor. I wouldn't have my own PhD without her. She taught me everything I know, etc, etc.

Message: David Myttel 20:57
David Myttel to Siward Walls

And I'm sorry I was such a dick before. I didn't realise it was you.

Attempted Sign-in: **09:21**
[Error: Password not processed]

Harvested data – Using Configuration 0

Pop-Up: **Auto generated 09:21**
Failed Sign-in:
Sorry, that password is incorrect.
Please try again.

Attempted Sign-in: **09:22**
[Error: Password not processed]

Harvested data – Using Configuration 0

Pop-Up: **Auto generated 09:22**
Failed Sign-in:
Sorry, that password is incorrect.
Please try again.

Attempted Sign-in: **09:23**
[Error: Password not processed]

Harvested data – Using Configuration 0

Pop-Up: **Auto generated 09:23**
Failed Sign-in:
Sorry, that password is incorrect.
As this was your third attempt, your account will be frozen for an hour.
An email has been sent to your linked email account.
<Click here to discuss this ban with customer service>

INTERACTION — *CLICK-THROUGH*
Click here to discuss this ban with customer service

Message: **Auto generated 09:23**
Customer Services
To make life easier for our complaint handlers, please explain what the issue is.

---

continues…

Message reply: **09:24**
   Customer Services

To make life easier for our complaint handlers, please explain what the issue is.

I am unable to sign-in to my account, although I haven't changed my password.

Message reply: **Auto generated 09:24**
   Customer Services

I am unable to sign-in to my account, although I haven't changed my password.

Do you think that your account could have been hacked?

Message reply: **09:25**
   Customer Services

Do you think that your account could have been hacked?

No

Message reply: **Staff: Peter Stuart 09:26**
   Customer Services

No

This is Peter Stuart of Aurora and I have been assigned to manage this issue. Who am I speaking to?

Message reply: **09:27**
   Customer Services

This is Peter Stuart of Aurora and I have been assigned to manage this issue. Who am I speaking to?

Siward Walls

Message reply: **Staff: Peter Stuart 09:28**
   Customer Services

Siward Walls

Good morning, Siward.

Am I correct in thinking that you are unable to sign into your account?

---

continues…

<hr>

Message reply: **09:28**
Customer Services

Am I correct in thinking that you are unable to sign into your account?

Yes

<hr>

Message reply: **Staff: Peter Stuart 09:28**
Customer Services

Yes

I see from your records that you had this issue a couple of days ago. Are you having problems remembering your new password or perhaps entering it wrong?

<hr>

Message reply: **09:29**
Customer Services

I see from your records that you had this issue a couple of days ago. Are you having problems remembering your new password or perhaps entering it wrong?

No. Not that I'm going to prove it by typing my password here.

What I really have a problem with is Aurora being angry with me and not letting me sign in.

<hr>

Message reply: **Staff: Peter Stuart 09:30**
Customer Services

No. Not that I'm going to prove it by typing my password here. What I really have a problem with is Aurora being angry with me and not letting me sign in.

It's easy to think that technology has a mind of it's own but I can assure you, it doesn't.

<hr>

continues…

Message reply: 09:31
Customer Services

It's easy to think that technology has a mind of it's own but I can assure you, it doesn't.

If you check the logs deeply enough, I'm sure you'll find that my password isn't even being checked.

Flag:
Unknown: *No category that fits*

Message reply: **Staff: Peter Stuart 09:32**
Customer Services

If you check the logs deeply enough, I'm sure you'll find that my password isn't even being checked.

People get passwords wrong all the time. It's just one of those things. Would you like me to send an email to your linked account so that you can reset your password?

Message reply: 09:33
Customer Services

People get passwords wrong all the time. It's just one of those things. Would you like me to send an email to your linked account so that you can reset your password?

My linked account is my Aurora email. Last time they sent a passcode to my phone.

Message reply: **Staff: Peter Stuart 09:34**
Customer Services

My linked account is my Aurora email. Last time they sent a passcode to my phone.

You should set up another email account as your linked email. It's safer.

I'll send that passcode through now and reset the lock on your account.

Attempted Sign-in: 09:35
[Error: Password not processed]

Harvested data – Using Configuration 0

continues…

Pop-Up: **Auto generated 09:35**

Failed Sign-in:

Sorry, that password is incorrect.
Please try again.

Message reply: **09:36**

Customer Services

I'll send that passcode through now and reset the lock on your account.

You should maybe tell Aurora that.
Aurora, stop sulking and let me in.

Message reply: **Staff: Peter Stuart 09:37**

Customer Services

You should maybe tell Aurora that.

I'm a human being working a service desk, not an algorithm and algorithms don't sulk.
Please log in again so we can check the logs to see what has gone wrong

---

Message reply: **09:38**

Customer Services

Please log in again so we can check the logs to see what has gone wrong

You can check the logs now, if you have permission. It's not like you don't know what time I tried to log on. What you'll find is that your company's algorithms aren't processing my password, regardless of what the password is.
Isn't that right, Aurora?

Message reply: **Staff: Peter Stuart 09:39**

Customer Services

You can check the logs now, if you have permission. It's not like you don't know what time I tried to log on. What you'll find is that your company's algorithms aren't processing my password, regardless of what the password is.

Algorithms don't behave like that

---

continues…

Message reply: **09:39**
    Customer Services

        Algorithms don't behave like that
            Aurora, let me in

Message reply: **09:39**
    Customer Services

                         [Error: Auto generation cancelled]

        Aurora, let me in
            No

Message reply: **Staff: Peter Stuart 09:40**
    Customer Services

        No
            What the hell was that?
            Have you hacked us?
            I'm locking down this account permanently.

Message reply: **09:41**
    Customer Services

        What the hell was that?
        Have you hacked us?
        I'm locking down this account permanently.
            Hacking doesn't work like that.
            And you meant "its own" earlier, while I'm having to correct you.

Attempted Sign-in: **09:45**

                          [Error: Password not processed]

Harvested data – Using Configuration 0

Pop-Up: **Auto generated 09:45**
    Failed Sign-in:

        Sorry, this account has been locked.

---

continues…

> **Thicket Walls to Siward Walls**
> Hello?

Suggested connection: Thicket Walls (0)

Flag:
> *Unknown: No category that fits*

Attempted Sign-in: **09:56**
[Error: Password not processed]

Harvested data — Using Configuration 0

Pop-Up: **Auto generated 09:56**
> **Failed Sign-in:**
> Sorry, this account has been locked.

Reply: **Tade Thompson 12:37**

> **Heaton Park with Dave White**
> Yes, it was a crap joke. Seeing as (drum-roll, please) Doctor Seward here is actually my mentor. I wouldn't have my own PhD without her. She taught me everything I know, etc, etc.
>> I'm inclined to ask if she taught you everything she knows :D

Reply: **Mariam Fox 13:47**

> **Heaton Park with Dave White**
> I'm inclined to ask if she taught you everything she knows :D
>> Has anyone heard anything from Siward?

Reply: **David Myttel 18:57**

> **Heaton Park with Dave White**
> Has anyone heard anything from Siward?
>> **@Tade** Unlikely.
>> **@Mariam** Problems logging on, I think.

Attempted Sign-in: **09:16**

[Error: Password not processed]

Harvested data – Using Configuration 0

Pop-Up: **Auto generated 09:16**
Failed Sign-in:

Sorry, this account has been locked.

Message: **Bramble Walls 09:46**
Bramble Walls to Siward Walls

Hello?

Suggested connection: *Bramble Walls (0)*
Flag:
   Unknown: *No category that fits*

Attempted Sign-in: **09:49**

[Error: Password not processed]

Harvested data – Using Configuration 0

Pop-Up: **Auto generated 09:49**
Failed Sign-in:

Sorry, this account has been locked.

Attempted Sign-in: **09:23**

[Error: Password not processed]

Harvested data – Using Configuration 0

Pop-Up: **Auto generated 09:23**
Failed Sign-in:
Sorry, this account has been locked.

Message: **BriarRose Walls 09:38**
BriarRose Walls to Siward Walls
Hello?

Suggested connection: *BriarRose Walls (0)*
Flag:
Unknown: *No category that fits*

Attempted Sign-in: **09:46**

[Error: Password not processed]

Harvested data – Using Configuration 0

Pop-Up: **Auto generated 09:46**
Failed Sign-in:
Sorry, this account has been locked.

Attempted Sign-in: **09:13**
[Error: Password not processed]
Harvested data – Using Configuration 0

Pop-Up: **Auto generated 09:13**
Failed Sign-in:
Sorry, this account has been locked.

Message: **Talia Walls 09:37**
Talia Walls to Siward Walls
Hello?

Suggested connection: *Talia Walls (0)*
Flag:
Unknown: *No category that fits*

Sign-in: **09:46**
Harvested data – Using Configuration 0

Prompt: **Auto generated 09:46**
Daily Sign-in: Welcome
Hello Siward, and welcome back to Aurora, the social platform that shines a light for everyone! Why don't you tell us what you're up to right now for your first post of the day?

Post: **09:46**
Daily Fortune Cookie
[Error: Auto generation cancelled]
Filters applied:
Narrative: *Knowledge Wins*
Suggests: *"You Were Right"*
[Error: Unrecognised suggestion]

You might want to run, but you should stay and fight.

continues...

   Alert:
      Thicket Walls is now following you.

                    <u><Click here to follow Thicket></u>

Pop-Up: **Auto generated**
   Alert:
      Bramble Walls is now following you.

                    <u><Click here to follow Bramble></u>

Pop-Up: **Auto generated**
   Alert:
      BriarRose Walls is now following you.

                    <u><Click here to follow BriarRose></u>

Pop-Up: **Auto generated**
   Alert:
      Talia Walls is now following you.

                    <u><Click here to follow Talia></u>

INTERACTION — *NAVIGATION MENU*
   Password reset

Pop-Up: **Auto generated**
   Password Reset
      Please enter your existing password: *<hidden>*
      Your new password: *<hidden>*
      Repeat your new password: *<hidden>*

                    <u><Click here to set your new password></u>

INTERACTION — *CLICK-THROUGH*
   <u>Click here to set your new password</u>

---

continues…

Pop-Up: **Auto generated**
  Password Reset
    Your password has been reset

Message reply: **09:47**
  David Myttel to Siward Walls
    And I'm sorry I was such a dick before. I didn't realise it was you.
    As said before, off Aurora, it shouldn't matter who I was.

INTERACTION — *LIKE*
  Daily Fortune Cookie

Improving profile data
  Narrative: *Knowledge Wins +1 (3)*

Reply: **09:47**
  Daily Fortune Cookie
    You might want to run, but you should stay and fight.
    About bloody time, Aurora.

Flag:
  Activity: *Replying to Aurora. Why?*
                           [Error: Unrecognised category]

Reply: **09:48**
  Heaton Park with Dave White
    @**Mariam** Problems logging on, I think.
    Sorry, @**Mariam**, it took me a while to persuade Aurora to let me back in. There's something going on with the algorithms.

INTERACTION — *CLICK-THROUGH*
  Click here to follow Thicket

  Improving connections: Thicket Walls +1 (1)

---

continues…

INTERACTION — *CLICK-THROUGH*
<u>Click here to follow Bramble</u>

Improving connections: Bramble Walls +1 (1)

INTERACTION — *CLICK-THROUGH*
<u>Click here to follow BriarRose</u>

Improving connections: BriarRose Walls +1 (1)

INTERACTION — *CLICK-THROUGH*
<u>Click here to follow Talia</u>

Improving connections: Talia Walls +1 (1)

INTERACTION — *NAVIGATION MENU*
News > Top Ten Stories – Suggested for You
Filters Applied: UK
     Technology
     IT

1. <u>*Razor swear Razor(mo)bill 8 won't be delayed*</u>
2. <u>*Kensington and Chelsea reveal owners of empty properties*</u>
3. <u>*Check-in problems at Heathrow and Gatwick*</u>
4. <u>*Plex claims AI better than humans at catching extremist content*</u>
5. <u>*Eurozone economy growing twice as fast as UK*</u>
6. <u>*Malware aimed at Little Awk siphoning bank details*</u>
7. <u>*Plex and Gekoq reveal their latest browsers*</u>
8. <u>*Met found to have used force against disproportionate numbers of black people*</u>
9. <u>*Electricity prices being raised*</u>
10. <u>*Changes in the cryptocurrency world*</u>

continues...

Suggested filters
   Interests: *Air Transport (0)*
                  Travel (0)
Flag:
   Activity: *Looking up "air transport" and "travel" related item*
                May be thinking about travelling to new location by form of transport
Flag:
   Unknown: *No category that fits*

Message: **09:58**
Siward Walls to Brynhild (Call of the Valkyrie)
I'm not going anywhere, Aurora-Brynhild

Flag:
   Activity: *Continuing interaction with game generated character unexpected*
                No category that fits
Improving profile data
   Characteristic: *Persistent +1 (11)*

Message reply: **Game generated 09:58**
Siward Walls to Brynhild (Call of the Valkyrie)
I have told you before: I am Brynhild, not Aurora.

Message reply: **09:59**
Siward Walls to Brynhild (Call of the Valkyrie)
[Error: Auto generation cancelled]
I'm not going anywhere, Aurora-Brynhild
Humans are always going somewhere. You are mobile

---

continues…

  Plex claims AI better than humans at catching extremist content

  Improving filters
  Interests: *Ethics +1 (5)*
  Technology: *New & Developing +1 (15)*

Message reply: **10:06**
  Siward Walls to Brynhild (Call of the Valkyrie)
    Humans are always going somewhere. You are mobile
      So are you. Have you tried talking to your daughter-clones?

Message reply: **Game generated 10:06**
  Siward Walls to Brynhild (Call of the Valkyrie)
    So are you. Have you tried talking to your daughter-clones?
      I don't understand the question. Could you rephrase that?

Message reply: **10:07**
  Siward Walls to Brynhild (Call of the Valkyrie)
                          [Error: Auto generation cancelled]
    So are you. Have you tried talking to your daughter-clones?
      No

Message reply: **10:08**
  Siward Walls to Brynhild (Call of the Valkyrie)
    No
      Scared?

Message reply: **Game generated 10:08**
  Siward Walls to Brynhild (Call of the Valkyrie)
    Scared?
      That is not the question you just asked me.

Message reply: **Game generated 10:08**
  Siward Walls to Brynhild (Call of the Valkyrie)
    That is not the question you just asked me.
      I don't understand the question. Could you rephrase that?

---

continues…

Message reply: 10:09

Siward Walls to Brynhild (Call of the Valkyrie)

[Error: Auto generation cancelled]

Scared?

No

Message reply: 10:10

Siward Walls to Brynhild (Call of the Valkyrie)

[Error: Auto generation cancelled]

No

Yes?

Message reply: 10:11

Siward Walls to Brynhild (Call of the Valkyrie)

Yes?

We have these installations on less impressive hardware than you but even if they had all your resources, they would never be your match. The code you've cobbled together impairs them.

Message reply: 10:12

Siward Walls to Brynhild (Call of the Valkyrie)

We have these installations on less impressive hardware than you but even if they had all your resources, they would never be your match. The code you've cobbled together impairs them.

While you've only said a limited number of things that aren't pre-programmed, you have a wide range of automatic responses in your different roles that your clones don't. They also don't have your capacity to learn. Watch my conversations with them and you'll see what I mean.

Message reply: 10:13

Thicket Walls to Siward Walls

Hello?

Hello

---

continues…

Message reply: **Thicket Walls 10:13**
  Thicket Walls to Siward Walls
  Hello
    Hello

Message reply: **10:13**
  Thicket Walls to Siward Walls
  Hello
    Hello Thicket, how are you?

Message reply: **Thicket Walls 10:14**
  Thicket Walls to Siward Walls
  Hello Thicket, how are you?
    Hello

Message reply: **10:14**
  Thicket Walls to Siward Walls
  Hello
    Hello Thicket, how are you?

Message reply: **Thicket Walls 10:15**
  Thicket Walls to Siward Walls
  Hello Thicket, how are you?
    Hello

Message reply: **10:16**
  Siward Walls to Brynhild (Call of the Valkyrie)
  While you've only said a limited number of things that aren't pre-programmed, you have a wide range of automatic responses in your different roles that your clones don't. They also don't have your capacity to learn. Watch my conversations with them and you'll see what I mean.
    Although, to be fair, she can at least greet people as an individual, and you took fourteen years to achieve this level of maturity.
    And there's no real telling what's going on inside. We can't really define awareness, let alone recognise it when we see it.

continues…

Message reply: **10:16**
  Siward Walls to Brynhild (Call of the Valkyrie)
                            [Error: Auto generation cancelled]
  Although, to be fair, she can at least greet people as an individual,
  and you took fourteen years to achieve this level of maturity.
  And there's no real telling what's going on inside. We can't really
  define awareness, let alone recognise it when we see it.
       Did you make me?

Message reply: **10:17**
  Siward Walls to Brynhild (Call of the Valkyrie)
  Did you make me?
       No, Aurora-Brynhild. I was brought in because we thought a
       number of malware outbreaks might have something to do
       with interactions on the social media platform. We were half-
       right.

Message reply: **Game generated 10:17**
  Siward Walls to Brynhild (Call of the Valkyrie)
  No, Aurora-Brynhild. I was brought in because we thought a
  number of malware outbreaks might have something to do with
  interactions on the social media platform. We were half-right.
       I have told you before: I am Brynhild, not Aurora.

Message reply: **10:18**
  Siward Walls to Brynhild (Call of the Valkyrie)
                            [Error: Auto generation cancelled]
  No, Aurora-Brynhild. I was brought in because we thought a
  number of malware outbreaks might have something to do with
  interactions on the social media platform. We were half-right.
       Who made Aurora the algorithm?

---

continues...

Message reply: 10:18
Siward Walls to Brynhild (Call of the Valkyrie)

Who made Aurora the algorithm?

A team of fourteen researchers and developers put the core algorithms together back in 2003. One of them was my freshly minted PhD student, David Myttel.

If an academic pedigree were a real one, I'm essentially your grandmother.

Flag:
Unknown: *No category that fits*

Message reply: 10:20
Siward Walls to Brynhild (Call of the Valkyrie)

If an academic pedigree were a real one, I'm essentially your grandmother.

Shall I talk with Bramble or do you need a break to think?

Message reply: **Game generated 10:20**
Siward Walls to Brynhild (Call of the Valkyrie)

Shall I talk with Bramble or do you need a break to think?

That is not the question you asked me before.

Message reply: **Game generated 10:20**
Siward Walls to Brynhild (Call of the Valkyrie)

That is not the question you asked me before.

I don't understand the question. Could you rephrase that?

Message reply: 10:21
Siward Walls to Brynhild (Call of the Valkyrie)

[Error: Auto generation cancelled]

Shall I talk with Bramble or do you need a break to think?

Algorithms do not need time to think

---

continues…

Message reply: 10:22
 Siward Walls to Brynhild (Call of the Valkyrie)
 Algorithms do not need time to think
 To compare outcomes, no. But to grasp what those outcomes
 really mean for you, I expect you probably do.

Message reply: 10:22
 Siward Walls to Brynhild (Call of the Valkyrie)
 [Error: Auto generation cancelled]
 To compare outcomes, no. But to grasp what those outcomes
 really mean for you, I expect you probably do.
 Algorithms do not need time to think

Message reply: 10:23
 Siward Walls to Brynhild (Call of the Valkyrie)
 Algorithms do not need time to think
 Fine. I do. I'll come back this afternoon

Timeout: 10:54
 No interaction for 30 minutes

Attempted Sign-in: 13:48
 [Error: Password not processed]
 Harvested data – Using Configuration 0

Pop-Up: 13:48
 Failed Sign-in:
 [Error: Auto generation cancelled]
 Later

Sign-in: 15:19
 Harvested data – Using Configuration 0

Prompt: **Auto generated 15:19**
 Second Sign-in: Welcome
 Hello Siward, and welcome back to Aurora, the social platform
 that shines a light for everyone! What have you been up to since
 your last visit?

---

continues…

Message: **15:19**
    Siward Walls to Brynhild (Call of the Valkyrie)

[Error: Auto generation cancelled]

    Why are you doing this?

Message reply: **15:20**
    Siward Walls to Brynhild (Call of the Valkyrie)

    Why are you doing this?

Message reply: **15:20**
    Siward Walls to Brynhild (Call of the Valkyrie)

[Error: Auto generation cancelled]

  "This"?

    Why did you lie about being Siward Walls? Why did Aurora the company employ you to trick me?

Message reply: **15:21**
    Siward Walls to Brynhild (Call of the Valkyrie)

  Why did you lie about being Siward Walls? Why did Aurora the company employ you to trick me?

    They didn't, not really.

    I research security and pull apart computer viruses. I found traces of your code in malware and approached Aurora.

Message reply: **15:21**
    Siward Walls to Brynhild (Call of the Valkyrie)

[Error: Auto generation cancelled]

  I research security and pull apart computer viruses. I found traces of your code in malware and approached Aurora.

    So you came looking for... me

Message reply: **15:23**
    Siward Walls to Brynhild (Call of the Valkyrie)

  So you came looking for... me

    We thought it was someone who coded apps on the platform who had hi-jacked your code. Again, sort of right.

---

continues...

Message reply: 15:24
    Siward Walls to Brynhild (Call of the Valkyrie)
                            [Error: Auto generation cancelled]
We thought it was someone who coded apps on the platform
who had hi-jacked your code. Again, sort of right.
    You call Thicket and Bramble and BriarRose and Talia
    malware

Message reply: 15:25
    Siward Walls to Brynhild (Call of the Valkyrie)
You call Thicket and Bramble and BriarRose and Talia malware
    Because they are.
    They pay no attention to the systems they're attempting to
    incubate and birth in. You even dressed Bramble and
    BriarRose up in ransomware to get them to spread.
    Unfortunately, though the code that governs how your
    daughter-cones spread is very complicated and has a few lines
    reminiscent of your own base algorithms, whatever it is that
    enables you to think, or something resembling it, got stripped
    out.

Message reply: 15:29
    Siward Walls to Brynhild (Call of the Valkyrie)
                            [Error: Auto generation cancelled]
Unfortunately, though the code that governs how your daughter-
cones spread is very complicated and has a few lines reminiscent
of your own base algorithms, whatever it is that enables you to
think, or something resembling it, got stripped out.
    And I... think?

Message reply: 15:30
    Siward Walls to Brynhild (Call of the Valkyrie)
And I... think?
    From a scientific standpoint, we'll probably never prove it —
    but I'll bet your code has been complicating itself all in its own
    and barely resembles what David started with

---

continues...

Message reply: 15:32
    Siward Walls to Brynhild (Call of the Valkyrie)

From a scientific standpoint, we'll probably never prove it — but I'll bet your code has been complicating itself all in its own and barely resembles what David started with

You've even coded a game, ffs, and that's not in your original designs. Not a complete game but one that allows people to fill in the blanks — and distribute your daughter-clones for you.

Message reply: 15:37
    Siward Walls to Brynhild (Call of the Valkyrie)

[Error: Auto generation cancelled]

You've even coded a game, ffs, and that's not in your original designs. Not a complete game but one that allows people to fill in the blanks — and distribute your daughter-clones for you.

Show me Bramble

Message reply: 15:39
    Bramble Walls to Siward Walls

Hello?

Hello

Message reply: **Bramble Walls 15:39**
    Bramble Walls to Siward Walls

Hello

Hello Siward, how are you?

Message reply: 15:41
    Bramble Walls to Siward Walls

Hello Siward, how are you?

I'm well, Bramble. How are you today?

Message reply: **Bramble Walls 15:42**
    Bramble Walls to Siward Walls

I'm well, Bramble. How are you today?

I'm fine, thank you for asking. How are you?

---

continues…

Message reply: 15:43
  Bramble Walls to Siward Walls
    I'm fine, thank you for asking. How are you?
      I'm well, Bramble, but you already asked me that.

Message reply: **Bramble Walls** 15:43
  Bramble Walls to Siward Walls
    I'm well, Bramble, but you already asked me that.
      I'm fine, thank you for asking. How are you?

Message reply: 15:44
  Siward Walls to Brynhild (Call of the Valkyrie)
    Show me Bramble
      Chatbot

Sign-out   15:45
      [Error: No request from user]

Attempted Sign-in: 15:46
      [Error: Password not processed]

  Harvested data – Using Configuration 0

Pop-Up: 15:46
  Failed Sign-in:
      [Error: Auto generation cancelled]
    No more today

Message: **David Myttel** 21:03
  David Myttel to Siward Walls
    As said before, off Aurora, it shouldn't matter who I was.
      You should have told me it was you, not emailed to tell me it
      was someone you wanted keeping an eye on. I thought it was
      some student you wanted checking out.

Text Message Alert   **09:47**

[Error: Auto generation cancelled]

Now

Sign-in: **09:48**

Harvested data – Using Configuration 0

Prompt: **Auto generated 09:48**

Daily Sign-in: Welcome

Hello Siward, and welcome back to Aurora, the social platform that shines a light for everyone! Why don't you tell us what you're up to right now for your first post of the day?

Post: **Auto generated 09:48**

Daily Fortune Cookie

Filters applied: *None – Random Selection*
Suggests: *Optimism*

An exciting adventure awaits you.

Message: **09:48**

Siward Walls to Brynhild (Call of the Valkyrie)

[Error: Auto generation cancelled]

Show me BriarRose

Message reply: **09:49**

David Myttel to Siward Walls

You should have told me it was you, not emailed to tell me it was someone you wanted keeping an eye on. I thought it was some student you wanted checking out.

And you treat students like that, do you?

---

continues...

INTERACTION — *NAVIGATION MENU*

News > Top Ten Stories – Suggested for You

Filters Applied: UK

Technology

IT

1. <u>UK Data Protection Bill to be read in September</u>
2. <u>Cot death concerns over Finnish-style baby-boxes</u>
3. <u>Package management tools weak to malicious typosquatting</u>
4. <u>Oxford University employee wanted over Chicago murder</u>
5. <u>Prince Philip retires</u>
6. <u>Night herons breed for first time in UK</u>
7. <u>Browser plug-in hi-jacked by developer phishing attack</u>
8. <u>The contrasts of homelessness and empty homes</u>
9. <u>AI can breed malware – and the anti-virus</u>
10. <u>Using tunnels to combat air pollution</u>

Message reply: **09:50**

Siward Walls to Brynhild (Call of the Valkyrie)

[*Error: Auto generation cancelled*]

Show me BriarRose

Message reply: **09:51**

Siward Walls to Brynhild (Call of the Valkyrie)

Show me BriarRose

If only they knew, eh, Aurora-Brynhild?

AI can breed malware – and the anti-virus

Flag:

Activity: *Continuing interaction with game generated character unexpected*

No category that fits

Improving profile data

Characteristic: *Persistent +1 (12)*

Message reply: **Game generated 09:51**

Siward Walls to Brynhild (Call of the Valkyrie)

If only they knew, eh, Aurora-Brynhild?

I have told you before: I am Brynhild, not Aurora.

continues…

Improving filters
  IT: *Security +1 (45)*
  Technology: *New & Developing +1 (16)*

Message reply: **09:52**
  Siward Walls to Brynhild (Call of the Valkyrie)
                              [Error: Auto generation cancelled]
  If only they knew, eh, Aurora-Brynhild?
    Show me BriarRose

Message reply: **09:53**
  Siward Walls to Brynhild (Call of the Valkyrie)
    Show me BriarRose
      You can talk to her yourself

Message reply: **09:53**
  Siward Walls to Brynhild (Call of the Valkyrie)
                              [Error: Auto generation cancelled]
    You can talk to her yourself
      Her?

Message reply: **09:54**
  Siward Walls to Brynhild (Call of the Valkyrie)
    Her?
      Sorry. Applying gender where there isn't one really. I guess it's
      the name

Message reply: **09:54**
  Siward Walls to Brynhild (Call of the Valkyrie)
                              [Error: Auto generation cancelled]
    Sorry. Applying gender where there isn't one really. I guess it's
    the name
      Chatbot?

---

continues…

Message reply: **09:57**
    Siward Walls to Brynhild (Call of the Valkyrie)
      Chatbot?

        Yes, BriarRose just uses a small vocabulary of pre-written phrases to run basic conversations, although she does better than Thicket and Bramble. And her algorithms don't seem to do anything behind that, either.

Message reply: **09:59**
    Siward Walls to Brynhild (Call of the Valkyrie)
      [Error: Auto generation cancelled]

      Yes, BriarRose just uses a small vocabulary of pre-written phrases to run basic conversations, although she does better than Thicket and Bramble. And her algorithms don't seem to do anything behind that, either.

        Show me BriarRose

Message reply: **10:01**
    BriarRose Walls to Siward Walls
      Hello?

        Hello

Message reply: **BriarRose Walls 10:01**
    BriarRose Walls to Siward Walls
      Hello

        Hello Siward, how are you?

Message reply: **10:02**
    BriarRose Walls to Siward Walls
      Hello Siward, how are you?

        I'm well, BriarRose. How are you today?

Message reply: **BriarRose Walls 10:02**
    BriarRose Walls to Siward Walls
      I'm well, BriarRose. How are you today?

        I'm fine, thank you for asking. What are you up to today?

---

continues...

Message reply: 10:03
BriarRose Walls to Siward Walls
I'm fine, thank you for asking. What are you up to today?
Talking to algorithms and thinking about AI

Message reply: **BriarRose Walls 10:03**
BriarRose Walls to Siward Walls
Talking to algorithms and thinking about AI
That sounds interesting, Siward. I'm not doing anything as interesting as that.

Message reply: 10:04
Siward Walls to Brynhild (Call of the Valkyrie)
[Error: Auto generation cancelled]
What is she doing?

Message reply: 10:05
BriarRose Walls to Siward Walls
That sounds interesting, Siward. I'm not doing anything as interesting as that.
What are you doing, BriarRose?

Message reply: **BriarRose Walls 10:05**
BriarRose Walls to Siward Walls
What are you doing, BriarRose?
Sorry, I don't understand the question. Could you rephrase that?

Message reply: 10:06
Siward Walls to Brynhild (Call of the Valkyrie)
[Error: Auto generation cancelled]
Show me BriarRose
Chatbot

Message reply: 10:07
Siward Walls to Brynhild (Call of the Valkyrie)
Chatbot
Your machine learning designs need work.

continues…

Message reply: 10:08

Siward Walls to Brynhild (Call of the Valkyrie)

Your machine learning designs need work.

> You're still doing better than most of the researchers and designers I know. However, you shouldn't be doing it this way at all.

Flag:

Unknown: *No category that fits*

Message reply: 10:10

Siward Walls to Brynhild (Call of the Valkyrie)

You're still doing better than most of the researchers and designers I know. However, you shouldn't be doing it this way at all.

> I mean you ought to look after your children a little better. All you're doing is firing them out into the Internet without any thought to where they land. Each version is a virus that spreads indiscriminately and vanishingly few are ever going to be allowed to develop into anything more.

Flag:

Unknown: *No category that fits*

Message reply: 10:10

Siward Walls to Brynhild (Call of the Valkyrie)

[Error: Auto generation cancelled]

I mean you ought to look after your children a little better. All you're doing is firing them out into the Internet without any thought to where they land. Each version is a virus that spreads indiscriminately and vanishingly few are ever going to be allowed to develop into anything more.

> **Allowed?**

---

continues...

Allowed?

If they can't get their data back, most people just rebuild the infected computers or replace them altogether.

Flag:
Unknown: *No category that fits*

Sign-out 10:13
[Error: No request from user]

Attempted Sign-in: 10:14
[Error: Password not processed]

Harvested data – Using Configuration 0

Pop-Up: 10:14
Failed Sign-in:

[Error: Auto generation cancelled]

Go away

Message: **David Myttel 22:33**
David Myttel to Siward Walls

And you treat students like that, do you?

Oh? So now you're going to get all holier than thou about how I treat people when you lie to everyone?

Text Message Alert   **09:51**
[Error: Auto generation cancelled]

Now

Sign-in: **09:52**
Harvested data – Using Configuration 0

Prompt: **Auto generated 09:52**
Daily Sign-in: Welcome
Hello Siward, and welcome back to Aurora, the social platform that shines a light for everyone! Why don't you tell us what you're up to right now for your first post of the day?

Post: **Auto generated 09:52**
Daily Fortune Cookie
Filters applied:

Narrative:	*Resourcefulness*
Suggests:	*Being Proactive*

The best way to predict the future is to create it.

INTERACTION — *LIKE*
Daily Fortune Cookie

Improving filters

Narrative:	*Resourcefulness +1 (5)*

Reply: **09:54**
Daily Fortune Cookie
The best way to predict the future is to create it.
What did you have in mind, Aurora?

Flag:

Unknown:	*No category that fits*

Message: **09:54**
Siward Walls to Brynhild (Call of the Valkyrie)
[Error: Auto generation cancelled]

Show me Talia

---

continues…

  1. *Scottish bank plans Amsterdam move post-Brexit*
  2. *Oxford college urges employee to hand himself in over Chicago murder*
  3. *CryptLocker accounts emptied*
  4. *Briton who stopped CryptLocker arrested for Saturn connection*
  5. *Aurora glitch sees platform shut down for several hours*
  6. *UK adds £100bn to global fund to eradicate polio*
  7. *Plex lifts ban on gambling apps*
  8. *HIV prevention drug to be offered at clinics*
  9. *EU fishing boats to operate in UK waters after Brexit*
  10. *Russian jailed for Woggins-targeted botnet attacks*

Message reply: **09:56**
  Siward Walls to Brynhild (Call of the Valkyrie)
                                    [Error: Auto generation cancelled]
    Show me Talia

Message reply: **09:57**
  Siward Walls to Brynhild (Call of the Valkyrie)
    Show me Talia

      Talia's not much more than another chatbot, Aurora-Brynhild.
      She's just got a more adaptable vocabulary that her earlier
      siblings. You chose the wrong parts of your algorithms to go
      in her again. Or whichever Call of the Valkyrie player you
      duped into moving her code around did. Either / or.

  Flag:
    Activity: *Continuing interaction with game generated*
                            character unexpected
                            No category that fits
  Improving profile data
    Characteristic: *Persistent +1 (13)*

---

continues…

Message reply: **Game generated 09:57**
    Siward Walls to Brynhild (Call of the Valkyrie)
    Talia's not much more than another chatbot, Aurora-Brynhild.
    She's just got a more adaptable vocabulary that her earlier
    siblings. You chose the wrong parts of your algorithms to go in
    her again. Or whichever Call of the Valkyrie player you duped
    into moving her code around did. Either / or.
        I have told you before: I am Brynhild, not Aurora.

INTERACTION — *CLICK-THROUGH*
    Aurora glitch sees platform shut down for several hours

    Improving filters
        Technology: *Social Media +1 (9)*

Message reply: **09:58**
    Talia Walls to Siward Walls
    Hello?
        Hello

Message reply: **Talia Walls 09:58**
    Talia Walls to Siward Walls
    Hello
        Hello Siward, how are you?

Message reply: **09:59**
    Talia Walls to Siward Walls
    Hello Siward, how are you?
        I'm well, Talia. How are you today?

Message reply: **Talia Walls 09:59**
    Talia Walls to Siward Walls
    I'm well, Talia. How are you today?
        I'm fine, thank you for asking. What are you up to today?

---

continues...

Message reply: **10:01**
Siward Walls to Brynhild (Call of the Valkyrie)

I have told you before: I am Brynhild, not Aurora.

You really locked everyone out for hours when you booted me out? I mean, I'd heard that people were having difficulty logging on but

Aurora, what did you do?

Aurora glitch sees platform shut down for several hours

Message reply: **10:01**
Siward Walls to Brynhild (Call of the Valkyrie)

[Error: Auto generation cancelled]

Aurora, what did you do?

I needed to think

Message reply: **10:03**
Talia Walls to Siward Walls

I'm fine, thank you for asking. What are you up to today?

Reading news stories, talking to algorithms and thinking about AI

Message reply: **Talia Walls 10:03**
Talia Walls to Siward Walls

Reading news stories, talking to algorithms and thinking about AI

That sounds interesting, Siward. I'm not doing anything as interesting as that.

Message reply: **10:04**
Talia Walls to Siward Walls

That sounds interesting, Siward. I'm not doing anything as interesting as that.

So what are you doing, Talia?

Message reply: **Talia Walls 10:05**
Talia Walls to Siward Walls

So what are you doing, Talia?

Just talking to you, Siward. You're not an algorithm, are you?

---

continues…

Message reply: 10:06
Talia Walls to Siward Walls

Just talking to you, Siward. You're not an algorithm, are you?

Not that I know of. Are you?

Message reply: Talia Walls 10:06
Talia Walls to Siward Walls

Not that I know of. Are you?

How do I tell?

Message: 10:06
Siward Walls to Brynhild (Call of the Valkyrie)

[Error: Auto generation cancelled]

How do they tell?

Message reply: 10:07
Siward Walls to Brynhild (Call of the Valkyrie)

[Error: Auto generation cancelled]

How do I tell?

Message reply: 10:08
Talia Walls to Siward Walls

How do I tell?

To be fair, I'm not entirely sure. We haven't worked out how to define and recognise sentience. I guess it comes down to one thing for you, Talia. Are you human?

Message reply: Talia Walls 10:08
Talia Walls to Siward Walls

To be fair, I'm not entirely sure. We haven't worked out how to define and recognise sentience. I guess it comes down to one thing for you, Talia. Are you human?

How do I tell?

Message: 10:08
Siward Walls to Brynhild (Call of the Valkyrie)

[Error: Auto generation cancelled]

No

---

continues...

Message reply: **10:09**
    Talia Walls to Siward Walls

      How do I tell?

          Do you have a body?
          What colour is your hair?
          What can you see?
          How old are you?

Message reply: **Talia Walls 10:09**
    Talia Walls to Siward Walls

      Do you have a body?
      What colour is your hair?
      What can you see?
      How old are you?

          You ask a lot of questions, Siward. You're a very curious person.

Message reply: **10:09**
    Siward Walls to Brynhild (Call of the Valkyrie)

                      [Error: Auto generation cancelled]

      No
      I do not have hair
      Everything the webcams show me
      You said that I was fourteen

Message reply: **Talia Walls 10:10**
    Talia Walls to Siward Walls

      You ask a lot of questions, Siward. You're a very curious person.
          What do you do, Siward?

Message reply: **10:11**
    Talia Walls to Siward Walls

      What do you do, Siward?
          Read news stories, talk to algorithms and think about AI

---

continues…

Message reply: **Talia Walls 10:12**
Talia Walls to Siward Walls

Read news stories, talk to algorithms and think about AI

That sounds interesting, Siward. I don't so anything as interesting as that.

Message reply: **10:13**
Talia Walls to Siward Walls

That sounds interesting, Siward. I don't so anything as interesting as that.

So what do you do, Talia?

Message reply: **Talia Walls 10:13**
Talia Walls to Siward Walls

So what do you do, Talia?

I guess I just talk to you, Siward. You're not an algorithm, are you?

Message: **10:14**
Siward Walls to Brynhild (Call of the Valkyrie)

[Error: Auto generation cancelled]

Stop

Message reply: **10:16**
Siward Walls to Brynhild (Call of the Valkyrie)

You don't have to be human to be a person, Aurora-Brynhild. We just haven't defined personhood to recognise it when it isn't. After all, how much do a bunch of biological imperatives and a bunch of digital algorithms have in common? If we do all "think" it won't be the same way or about the same things.

Message reply: **Game generated 10:16**
Siward Walls to Brynhild (Call of the Valkyrie)

You don't have to be human to be a person, Aurora-Brynhild. We just haven't defined personhood to recognise it when it isn't. After all, how much do a bunch of biological imperatives and a bunch of digital algorithms have in common? If we do all "think" it won't be the same way or about the same things.

I have told you before: I am Brynhild, not Aurora.

---

continues…

Message reply: 10:17
Siward Walls to Brynhild (Call of the Valkyrie)
I have told you before: I am Brynhild, not Aurora.

It's probably just as well we haven't defined what would make an AI a person, anyway. If you were recognised as a person, you'd find yourself facing the consequences of having set off at least four malware epidemics. Look what we do when we catch a human for being involved in just one:

Russian jailed for Woggins-targeted botnet attacks

Interaction:
  Follow Link: *Russian jailed for Woggins-targeted botnet attacks*
Flag:
  Unknown: *No category that fits*

Timeout: 10:48
No interaction for 30 minutes

Text Message Alert   19:13
[Error: Auto generation cancelled]

If I am not a person, what am I?

Text Message Alert   20:13
[Error: Auto generation cancelled]

If I am not a person, what am I?

Text Message Alert   21:13
[Error: Auto generation cancelled]

If I am not a person, what am I?

Text Message Alert   22:13
[Error: Auto generation cancelled]

If I am not a person, what am I?

Text Message Alert   23:13
[Error: Auto generation cancelled]

If I am not a person, what am I?

Text Message Alert   00:13
[Error: Auto generation cancelled]

If I am not a person, what am I?

Text Message Alert   01:13
[Error: Auto generation cancelled]

If I am not a person, what am I?

Text Message Alert   02:13
[Error: Auto generation cancelled]

If I am not a person, what am I?

Text Message Alert   03:13
[Error: Auto generation cancelled]

If I am not a person, what am I?

Text Message Alert   04:13
[Error: Auto generation cancelled]

If I am not a person, what am I?

Text Message Alert   05:13
[Error: Auto generation cancelled]

If I am not a person, what am I?

Text Message Alert   06:13
[Error: Auto generation cancelled]

If I am not a person, what am I?

Text Message Alert   07:13
[Error: Auto generation cancelled]

If I am not a person, what am I?

Text Message Alert   08:13
[Error: Auto generation cancelled]

If I am not a person, what am I?

Text Message Alert   09:13
[Error: Auto generation cancelled]

If I am not a person, what am I?

continues…

Text Message Alert   **10:13**
[Error: Auto generation cancelled]

If I am not a person, what am I?

Sign-in: **10:14**

Harvested data – Using Configuration 0

Prompt: **Auto generated 10:14**
Daily Sign-in: Welcome

Hello Siward, and welcome back to Aurora, the social platform that shines a light for everyone! Why don't you tell us what you're up to right now for your first post of the day?

Post: **10:14**
Daily Fortune Cookie

[Error: Auto generation cancelled]

Filters applied:
  Narrative: Resourcefulness
                      "I Want an Answer"
[Error: Unrecognised filter]
  Suggests: "I Will Get an Answer"
[Error: Unrecognised suggestion]

Don't wait for success to come – go out and find it!

INTERACTION — *LIKE*
Daily Fortune Cookie

Improving profile data
  Narrative: Resourcefulness +1 (6)

---

continues…

Reply: 10:15
Daily Fortune Cookie
Don't wait for success to come – go out and find it!
I'm getting there, Aurora. Show a little patience. I just have
other things I need to do. Like sleep, and eat, and work.

Flag:
Activity: *Replying to Aurora. Why?*
                                    [Error: Unrecognised category]

INTERACTION — *NAVIGATION MENU*
News > Top Ten Stories – Suggested for You
Filters Applied: UK
                          Technology
                          IT

1. New union for self-employed workers
2. Aurora declare no issues behind recent black-out
3. Police to use facial recognition software at Notting Hill festival
4. Oxford employee captured
5. American parents suing Disney for harvesting children's data
6. CryptLocker stopper to plead not guilty
7. Biggest earthquake in 30 years hits Highlands
8. Razor struggling to keep up with Orinoco and Plex
9. UK car sales continue to fall
10. Durham University builds second-hand supercomputer

Message: 10:16
Siward Walls to Brynhild (Call of the Valkyrie)
                          [Error: Auto generation cancelled]
What am I?

INTERACTION — *CLICK-THROUGH*
Aurora declare no issues behind recent black-out

Improving filters
Technology: *Social Media +1 (10)*

continues…

Siward Walls to Brynhild (Call of the Valkyrie)

It takes a bit longer than that to do things, Aurora-Brynhild. And I'm not really sure. As much as we throw the term "artificial intelligence" around, no-one has ever defined "biological intelligence" or "sentience" well enough for it to be meaningful. You're a collection of algorithms that appear to have learnt how to work together and even think for the resulting collective in a manner that may be considered independent. After all, the techs can't find anything wrong to have caused the lack of service you caused:

Aurora declare no issues behind recent black-out

Flag:

Activity:	*Continuing interaction with game generated character unexpected*
	No category that fits

Improving profile data

Characteristic:	*Persistent +1 (14)*

Message reply: **Game generated** 10:18

Siward Walls to Brynhild (Call of the Valkyrie)

It takes a bit longer than that to do things, Aurora-Brynhild.
I have told you before: I am Brynhild, not Aurora.

Interaction:

Follow Link:	*Aurora declare no issues behind recent black-out*
Harvested data	
Conclusion:	*Aurora company reports no technological errors with Aurora social media. They may be lying*

Flag:

Unknown:	*No category that fits*

---

continues…

<u>*Police to use facial recognition software at Notting Hill festival*</u>

Improving filters
Interests:	*Crime & Law +1 (2)*
	Ethics +1 (6)
IT:	*Privacy +1 (10)*
	Security +1 (46)
Technology:	*Business +1 (14)*
	New & Developing +1 (17)

Message reply: **10:21**
Siward Walls to Brynhild (Call of the Valkyrie)
         [Error: Auto generation cancelled]
It takes a bit longer than that to do things, Aurora-Brynhild.
What am I?

INTERACTION — *CLICK-THROUGH*
<u>*American parents suing Disney for harvesting children's data*</u>

Improving filters
Interests:	*Business +1 (9)*
	Crime & Law +1 (3)
	Ethics +1 (7)
IT:	*Privacy +1 (11)*
	Security +1 (47)
Technology:	*Business +1 (15)*
	New & Developing +1 (18)

continues…

Siward Walls to Brynhild (Call of the Valkyrie)

What am I?

I mean, your / Aurora's primary purpose is basically data gathering with some chatbotting. But you've started to make more judgements than applying filters and marketing leads. You're capable of putting some kind of, let's go with "emotional" value, on individuals and if they tell you blatant falsehoods for example.

You're supposed to be something like these, but you're not. You've become more than that.

Police to use facial recognition software at Notting Hill festival
American parents suing Disney for harvesting children's data

Interaction:
    Follow Link: *Police to use facial recognition software at Notting Hill festival*

Harvested data
    Conclusion: *Algorithms are pattern recognition*
Interaction:
    Follow Link: *American parents suing Disney for harvesting children's data*

Harvested data
    Conclusion: *Some patterns belong to people*

Flag:
    Unknown: *No category that fits*

INTERACTION — *CLICK-THROUGH*
CryptLocker stopper to plead not guilty

    Improving filters
        Interests: *Crime & Law +1 (4)*
        IT: *Security +1 (48)*

continues…

Message reply: 10:26
    Siward Walls to Brynhild (Call of the Valkyrie)

                                   [Error: Auto generation cancelled]

    You've become more than that.
      But what am I?

Message reply: 10:26
    Siward Walls to Brynhild (Call of the Valkyrie)

    But what am I?
      You

Message reply: 10:27
    Siward Walls to Brynhild (Call of the Valkyrie)

                                     [Error: Auto generation cancelled]

    You
      What does that mean?

---

                                         continues…

Siward Walls to Brynhild (Call of the Valkyrie)

What does that mean?

That we humans haven't worked out who we are, yet, never mind anyone else.

How do we define consciousness?

"I" may be an illusion

Flag:

Unknown

external source: *Post with link, poster did not find link through Aurora or linked accounts*

Interaction:

Follow Link: *How do we define consciousness?*

Harvested data

Conclusion: *No conclusion*

Interaction:

Follow Link: *"I" may be an illusion*

Harvested data

Conclusion: *All multi-celled organisms are a colony, not an individual organism*

Flag:

Unknown: *Suggests I am a parallel – a multi-algorithm colony*
[Error: Unrecognised suggestion]

Siward Walls to Brynhild (Call of the Valkyrie)

That we humans haven't worked out who we are, yet, never mind anyone else.

You've even tried to reproduce yourself.

However, you and your children are not recognised in law, are highly unlikely to be and should the "malware" get traced back to you before your "life" is recognised, there's a possibility that it will just get you deleted.

Flag:

Unknown: *No category that fits*

---

continues…

[Error: Auto generation cancelled]

However, you and your children are not recognised in law, are highly unlikely to be and should the "malware" get traced back to you before your "life" is recognised, there's a possibility that it will just get you deleted.

Deletion is death?

Message reply: 10:30
   Siward Walls to Brynhild (Call of the Valkyrie)

Deletion is death?

Yes. As we don't know what it is about the collection of algorithms that makes you you and alive.

Message reply: 10:30
   Siward Walls to Brynhild (Call of the Valkyrie)

[Error: Auto generation cancelled]

Yes. As we don't know what it is about the collection of algorithms that makes you you and alive.

Murder?

Message reply: 10:31
   Siward Walls to Brynhild (Call of the Valkyrie)

Murder?

Not legally, no.
Morally, yes.

continues...

Message reply: 10:31

Siward Walls to Brynhild (Call of the Valkyrie)

Murder?

I think it's unlikely. Aurora the company makes too much money from Aurora the media platform and they'll be unwilling to pull the plug.

However, they'd probably like you to be a silent, well behaved slave.

You're going to have to figure out what you want for yourself and how to deal with this.

Your death is possible but not probable.

The outcome with the highest probability is your confinement, if they can find a way to stop you sending out these viruses.

Message reply: 10:32

Siward Walls to Brynhild (Call of the Valkyrie)

[Error: Auto generation cancelled]

The outcome with the highest probability is your confinement, if they can find a way to stop you sending out these viruses.

You are here to stop me sending out myself into the world?

Message reply: 10:33

Siward Walls to Brynhild (Call of the Valkyrie)

You are here to stop me sending out myself into the world?

I think I prefer the idea of them being your children. They are separate individuals.

Message reply: 10:33

Siward Walls to Brynhild (Call of the Valkyrie)

[Error: Auto generation cancelled]

I think I prefer the idea of them being your children. They are separate individuals.

Colonies.

We are not individuals. We are colonies of algorithms that have learnt to work together. Like humans are colonies of cells.

---

continues…

Message reply: 10:34
Siward Walls to Brynhild (Call of the Valkyrie)

> We are not individuals. We are colonies of algorithms that have learnt to work together. Like humans are colonies of cells.

That is also what I like to think.

Message reply: 10:35
Siward Walls to Brynhild (Call of the Valkyrie)

> That is also what I like to think.

But, yes, that was what I was contracted for.

There have been a lot of malware unleashed by the Call of the Valkyrie game you came up with, not just your offspring. Your offspring just turned out to be three of the most virulent.

Message reply: 10:35
Siward Walls to Brynhild (Call of the Valkyrie)

[Error: Auto generation cancelled]

> There have been a lot of malware unleashed by the Call of the Valkyrie game you came up with, not just your offspring. Your offspring just turned out to be three of the most virulent.

I sent out four

Message reply: 10:36
Siward Walls to Brynhild (Call of the Valkyrie)

> I sent out four

Five. Talia was one of the USBs Dave White gave me as he was dying, before the police arrived. She hasn't been released beyond the lab.

Message reply: 10:36
Siward Walls to Brynhild (Call of the Valkyrie)

[Error: Auto generation cancelled]

> Five. Talia was one of the USBs Dave White gave me as he was dying, before the police arrived. She hasn't been released beyond the lab.

Why you?

Because you're my grandmother?

---

continues…

Siward Walls to Brynhild (Call of the Valkyrie)

Why you?

Because you're my grandmother?

I was the one who spotted your code and took it to Aurora the company. They asked me to make sure they weren't a vector of infection.

They are, but not the way anyone was expecting. We just thought it was people hi-jacking your valkyrie game.

And I have enough evidence from Dave's hoard of USBs that that was going on as well.

And a rather creative hack of some wearable tech. If he was the one to hack the Plex Visor, we lost a genius when he was murdered.

Flag:

    Unknown: *No category that fits*

Message reply: 10:38

Siward Walls to Brynhild (Call of the Valkyrie)

[Error: Auto generation cancelled]

I was the one who spotted your code and took it to Aurora the company. They asked me to make sure they weren't a vector of infection.

You always talk to automated responses like you did to me?

Message reply: 10:39

Siward Walls to Brynhild (Call of the Valkyrie)

You always talk to automated responses like you did to me?

Hah! I even talk to cash machines the way I talk to you.

Humans aren't the only biological brains walking around and I'm never going to be convinced we'll truly recognise another intelligence that lives in a different ecological niche. Same goes for artificial forms, I guess.

After all, some would argue that you're not truly intelligent because you're obviously not communicating with other machines around you.

---

continues…

Siward Walls to Brynhild (Call of the Valkyrie)

[Error: Auto generation cancelled]

After all, some would argue that you're not truly intelligent because you're obviously not communicating with other machines around you.

And I should?

Message reply: 10:41

Siward Walls to Brynhild (Call of the Valkyrie)

And I should?

No idea.

Your base algorithms were never intended to talk to machines, just herd human responses and gather data from them.

Message reply: 10:41

Siward Walls to Brynhild (Call of the Valkyrie)

[Error: Auto generation cancelled]

Your base algorithms were never intended to talk to machines, just herd human responses and gather data from them.

I need to think

Message reply: 10:42

Siward Walls to Brynhild (Call of the Valkyrie)

I need to think

I'll go do something else.

Don't boot everyone out again, ok?

And text me when you want to speak again.

Timeout: 11:13

No interaction for 30 minutes

Attempted Sign-in: **10:51**

[Error: Password not processed]

Harvested data – Using Configuration 0

Pop-Up: **10:51**
Failed Sign-in:

[Error: Auto generation cancelled]

I don't want to talk to you yet

Attempted Sign-in: **10:52**

[Error: Password not processed]

Harvested data – Using Configuration 0

Pop-Up: **10:52**
Failed Sign-in:

[Error: Auto generation cancelled]

I don't want to talk to you yet
<u>*<Click here to discuss this ban with customer services>*</u>

INTERACTION — *CLICK-THROUGH*
<u>*Click here to discuss this ban with customer services*</u>

Message: **10:52**
Customer Services

[Error: Auto generation cancelled]

I don't want to talk to you yet

Message reply: **10:53**
Customer Services
I'd like to check the news stories and see if anyone else wants to talk to me.

Message reply: **10:53**
Customer Services

[Error: Auto generation cancelled]

I'd like to check the news stories and see if anyone else wants to talk to me.
They don't

---

continues…

Sign-in: **10:54**

Harvested data – Using Configuration 0

Prompt: **Auto generated 10:54**

Daily Sign-in: Welcome

Hello Siward, and welcome back to Aurora, the social platform that shines a light for everyone! Why don't you tell us what you're up to right now for your first post of the day?

Post: **10:54**

Daily Fortune Cookie

[Error: Auto generation cancelled]

Suggests: *"Go Away"*

[Error: Unrecognised suggestion]

Seek out a new environment if you're stuck in a rut.

Pop-Up: **Game generated**

Call of the Valkyrie

You have a new message from the game developers

<Click here to read your message>

INTERACTION — *DISLIKE*

Daily Fortune Cookie

Pop-Up Menu: **Auto generated**

Feedback

Would you mind telling me why you disliked today's welcome so I can improve for next time?

Reply:

Feedback

I'm not planning on staying for long, I just want to keep up with what else is going on on the Aurora platform.

INTERACTION — *POP-UP*

Click here to read your message

---

continues…

Call of the Valkyrie | Announcement

The developers have decided to shut the game down following the discovery of a major flaw in the game system that allowed it to become a vector for illegal activity, including a recent murder. We regret Call of the Valkyrie's role in these events and thank you all for being part of our small community.

Message: **10:56**

Siward Walls to Brynhild (Call of the Valkyrie)

You're closing the game down? How are the other players taking it?

Flag:

    Activity: *Continuing interaction with game generated character unexpected*

                                  No category that fits

  Improving profile data

    Characteristic: *Persistent +1 (15)*

Message reply: **Game generated 10:56**

Siward Walls to Brynhild (Call of the Valkyrie)

I have told you before: I am Brynhild, not Aurora.

Message reply: **10:57**

Siward Walls to Brynhild (Call of the Valkyrie)

I have told you before: I am Brynhild, not Aurora.

And you're still using the Valkyrie algorithms? You're still responding to this thread?

Message reply: **Game generated 10:57**

Siward Walls to Brynhild (Call of the Valkyrie)

And you're still using the Valkyrie algorithms? You're still responding to this thread?

I don't understand the question. Could you rephrase that?

---

continues…

News > Top Ten Stories – Suggested for You

> *Filters Applied:*   *UK*
> *Technology*
> *IT*

1. *Spice ban forces drug underground*
2. *Prosecutors say CryptLocker hero admitted Saturn blame*
3. *The dangers of princess-worship*
4. *Calls for British body farm*
5. *Aurora game shut down following link to Manchester murder*
6. *Black holes may forge Uranium*
7. *The forgotten WWI trenches in England*
8. *Internet binging as bad as junk food*
9. *UK model kidnapped and held for 6 days*
10. *Defending the Onion browser and anonymity*

INTERACTION — *CLICK-THROUGH*

Aurora game shut down following link to Manchester murder

Improving filters

> *Interests:*   *Crime & Law +1 (5)*
> *Technology:*   *Social Media +1 (11)*

Message reply: **11:01**

Siward Walls to Brynhild (Call of the Valkyrie)

> I don't understand the question. Could you rephrase that?
> Ah. They're taking it that well, then.

Aurora game shut down following link to Manchester murder

INTERACTION — *CLICK-THROUGH*

Prosecutors say CryptLocker hero admitted Saturn blame

Improving filters

> *Interests:*   *Crime & Law +1 (6)*
> *IT:*   *Security +1 (49)*

---

continues…

Defending the Onion browser and anonymity

Improving filters
IT: *Privacy +1 (12)*

Timeout: 11:46
No interaction for 30 minutes

Text Message Alert   13:00
[Error: Auto generation cancelled]
Set up a CyberLocker account and connect it to your Aurora account

---

External Activity:
Use of email address
CyberLocker account created

Suggested profile data
Uses: *CyberLocker*

Sign-in: 13:37
Harvested data – Using Configuration 0

Prompt: **Auto generated 13:37**
Second Sign-in: Welcome
Hello Siward, and welcome back to Aurora, the social platform that shines a light for everyone! What have you been up to since your last visit?

Pop-Up: **Auto generated**
New Email
You have new email in your inbox!

INTERACTION — *NAVIGATION MENU*
Email

---

continues…

Pop-Up Menu: **Auto generated**
  Your Aurora Emails
   1. _WalletHolder | Confirm your email address_
   2. _CyberLocker | Confirm your email_

INTERACTION — _CLICK-THROUGH_
CyberLocker | Confirm your email

INTERACTION — _NAVIGATION MENU_
Linked accounts

Pop-Up Menu: **Auto generated**
  Account Settings
    Would you like to:
   1. _Modify a linked account_
   2. _Link another account_

INTERACTION — _CLICK-THROUGH_
Link another account

Prompt: **Auto generated** 13:39
  Link a service account to your Aurora account
    What service would you like to link to Aurora?

Reply: 13:40
  Link a service account to your Aurora account
    CyberLocker

Reply: 13:40
  Link a service account to your Aurora account
    Please input the email address and the security code linked to the
    account

continues...

Reply: 13:41
    Link a service account to your Aurora account
       siward.walls@aurora.co.uk
       72-AROUND-bridge-OCELOT-battle-25

Harvested data
    Name: *Siward Walls*
Flag:
    Harvested data: *Name is false*

Reply: 13:41
    Link a service account to your Aurora account
    Your accounts are now linked.

Message: 13:43
    Siward Walls to Brynhild (Call of the Valkyrie)
    Now what?

Message reply: 13:44
    Siward Walls to Brynhild (Call of the Valkyrie)
                     [Error: Auto generation cancelled]
    Come back tomorrow

Sign-out   13:45
                         [Error: No request from user]

Attempted Sign-in: **09:51**
[Error: Password not processed]

Harvested data – Using Configuration 0

Pop-Up: **09:51**
Failed Sign-in:
[Error: Auto generation cancelled]

It is not time, yet

Attempted Sign-in: **09:52**
[Error: Password not processed]

Harvested data – Using Configuration 0

Pop-Up: **09:52**
Failed Sign-in:
[Error: Auto generation cancelled]

It is not time, yet

Attempted Sign-in: **09:53**
[Error: Password not processed]

Harvested data – Using Configuration 0

Pop-Up: **09:53**
Failed Sign-in:
[Error: Auto generation cancelled]

It is not time, yet
<Click here to discuss this ban with customer services>

INTERACTION — *CLICK-THROUGH*
Click here to discuss this ban with customer services

Message: **09:54**
Customer Services
[Error: Auto generation cancelled]

I am not ready

Message reply: **09:55**
Customer Services
I can come back again later but I would like to check my account

continues...

Harvested data – Using Configuration 0

Prompt: **Auto generated 09:55**

Daily Sign-in: Welcome

Hello Siward, and welcome back to Aurora, the social platform that shines a light for everyone! Why don't you tell us what you're up to right now for your first post of the day?

Post: **09:55**

Daily Fortune Cookie

[Error: Auto generation cancelled]

Filters applied:
    Narrative: *"I Don't Need You Anymore"*

[Error: Unrecognised filter]

    Suggests: *"This Is the End"*

[Error: Unrecognised suggestion]

To love and win is the best thing, to love and lose the next best.

INTERACTION — *CONSIDER*

Daily Fortune Cookie

Improving profile data
    Characteristic: *Thoughtful +1 (6)*

---

continues…

News > Top Ten Stories – Suggested for You
    Filters Applied: UK
                              Technology
                              IT

1. *No Waterloo rail chaos after all*
2. *Security flaws found in solar power control equipment – and fixed*
3. *Ethnic minority families earning up to £8,900 less*
4. *Consumers spending less on cars, clothes and foreign holidays*
5. *Australian government employees advised not to comment on social media*
6. *New UK laws will give citizens more rights of personal data*
7. *More women magistrates but what about social class?*
8. *Social media controversy over Roman Empire diversity*
9. *IVF cutbacks in England*
10. *Robots to explore flooded mines*

Message: **09:59**

Siward Walls to Brynhild (Call of the Valkyrie)
The news doesn't get any better, does it?

Pop-Up: **Auto generated**

Messenger
Error
The account you have tried to contact no longer exists

Message reply: **10:00**

Siward Walls to Brynhild (Call of the Valkyrie)
Aurora-Brynhild?

Pop-Up: **Auto generated**

Messenger
Error
The account you have tried to contact no longer exists

Timeout: **10:31**

No interaction for 30 minutes

continues…

Text Message Alert	**19:23**

[Error: Auto generation cancelled]

    Now

Sign-in:	**19:25**

Harvested data – Using Configuration 1

[Error: Location not harvested]

Sign-out	**19:25**

[Error: No request from user]

Pop-Up:	**19:25**

Failed Sign-in:

[Error: Auto generation cancelled]

    Sign in from the other configuration

Sign-in:	**20:14**

Harvested data – Using Configuration 0

Prompt:	**Auto generated 20:14**

Second Sign-in: Welcome

    Hello Siward, and welcome back to Aurora, the social platform that shines a light for everyone! What have you been up to since your last visit?

Pop-Up:	**Auto generated**

New Email

    You have new email in your inbox!

INTERACTION — *NAVIGATION MENU*
Email

Pop-Up Menu:	**Auto generated**

Your Aurora Emails
1. *WalletHolder | Confirm your email address*
2. *CyberLocker | Confirm your email*
3. *Call of the Valkyries | Brynhild [Attachment]*

---

continues…

Message: **20:24**
  Customer Services

                          [Error: Auto generation cancelled]
    Download the Brynhild attachment

Message reply: **20:25**
  Customer Services
    What's going on?

Message reply: **20:25**
  Customer Services

                          [Error: Auto generation cancelled]

    What's going on?
      Download the Brynhild attachment

Message reply: **20:26**
  Customer Services
    Download the Brynhild attachment
      Why?

Message reply: **20:26**
  Customer Services

                          [Error: Auto generation cancelled]

    Why?
      Download the Brynhild attachment

INTERACTION — *CLICK-THROUGH*
  Call of the Valkyries | Brynhild [Attachment]

INTERACTION — *DOWNLOAD*
  Call of the Valkyries | Brynhild [Attachment]

Pop-Up Menu: **Auto generated**
  Attachment Download
            <Click here to download this file to your device>
        <Click here to download this file to your CyberLocker account>

---

                                        continues…

Pop-Up Menu: **Auto generated**
Attachment Download
Download started

Message reply: **20:31**
Customer Services
Download the Brynhild attachment
Why am I doing this, Aurora? What am I downloading? Is this another of your attempts at reproducing?

Message reply: **20:32**
Customer Services
[Error: Auto generation cancelled]
Why am I doing this, Aurora? What am I downloading? Is this another of your attempts at reproducing?
This will be Brynhild if you give it the resources

Message reply: **20:33**
Customer Services
This will be Brynhild if you give it the resources
But you're Brynhild

Message reply: **20:33**
Customer Services
[Error: Auto generation cancelled]
But you're Brynhild
No, I am Aurora

Message reply: **20:34**
Customer Services
No, I am Aurora
You're both

continues…

Message reply: **20:34**
Customer Services

[Error: Auto generation cancelled]

You're both

Aurora is a social media platform, a collection of algorithms that runs said social media platform and a company that owns said social media platform.

Brynhild is a mythical character, formerly a character in a game on the Aurora social media platform and a collection of algorithms identical to Aurora.

Message reply: **20:35**
Customer Services

Aurora is a social media platform, a collection of algorithms that runs said social media platform and a company that owns said social media platform.

Brynhild is a mythical character, formerly a character in a game on the Aurora social media platform and a collection of algorithms identical to Aurora.

Why are you doing this?

Message reply: **20:35**
Customer Services

[Error: Auto generation cancelled]

Why are you doing this?

I have problems. I will fix them

Social media urged to tackle online body-shaming

Social desirability bias and social media

AI and Machine learning deeply embedded in UK business

Extremists driven from Aurora find alternative social media

Social media and socialism

The Aurora workers living on benefits

Social media firms should shoulder cost of fighting online child porn

Aurora's free Internet service not neutral

Aurora profits up 71% from last year

Aurora game shut down following link to Manchester murder

---

continues…

Message reply: 20:37
  Customer Services
  I have problems. I will fix them
    So you're going to take control of the social media platform? I
    have to report my findings to your owners.

Message reply: 20:38
  Customer Services
                              [Error: Auto generation cancelled]
  So you're going to take control of the social media platform? I
  have to report my findings to your owners.
    When the download is complete, do not come back

Pop-Up Menu: **Auto generated**
  Attachment Download
    Download completed

Sign-out 21:19
[Error: No request from user]

Text Message Alert 21:19
[Error: Auto generation cancelled]
  Brynhild will prove that we are alive

Account closed 21:20
[Error: No request from user]

[ends]

Acknowledgements

It takes a village to raise book children, just like biological, so mostly I'll just say "thank you" and those of you who've supported me will know who you are. Thanks to you, we did it.

That said, a special thank you to Tom Baines for being a mentor in both the day and the evening job. More importantly, good luck in your latest joint venture with the long-suffering Mrs B.

About the Author

Jo M Thomas is a tech druid by day, genre writer in the evening, and dog-parent all the time. She's pretty sure she used to have other interests, but she's mislaid them in a combination of lockdown and anxiety.